HORSE WITH NO NAME

A Town Called Horse Historical Mystery

ALEXANDRA AMOR

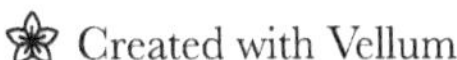

For Lorraine

HORSE WITH NO NAME

CHAPTER ONE

Millie Jones' hand was like a vice around Constable Jack Merrick's wrist. Julia understood how he felt; her own wrist was being crushed by Millie's other claw.

The schoolhouse where Julia worked was doubling as a dance hall this evening because it was the only building in town that could hold most of the inhabitants at once. This was Julia's first dance in Horse since she'd arrived six weeks earlier. She was having a lively chat with one of her student's parents when the mayor's wife, Millicent Jones, dragged Constable Jack Merrick over.

"Come on now, you two," Millie said. "Don't be shy. Have a dance with each other. That's why we're here."

Merrick looked at Julia with a mixture of terror and mortification in his eyes. She had never seen the big policeman look afraid of anything, and here he was being reduced to a quivering mess by the suggestion of a dance.

"I'm a terrible dancer," he said to Julia, almost pleading.

Julia didn't get a chance to let him off the hook.

"Nonsense!" Millie shrilled, "It's a wee country dance. You'll have no trouble, Constable." Though Millie never lifted a hand unless she had to, she seemed to have the strength of three men; she managed to pull Julia and Merrick together by their arms and push them toward the dance floor.

As they reached the floor Merrick self-consciously wiped his palms on his trousers and then held them out to Julia. His expression was pained. "I apologize in advance," he said, "I wasn't being modest before. I really am an awful dancer."

"I'm sure you'll be fine." Julia smiled at him reassuringly and took his hands.

Unfortunately, he wasn't wrong. His movements were stiff and awkward, and he obviously wasn't familiar with the waltz. She could hear him counting under his breath, which made her want to laugh. They moved around the floor, occasionally bumping into other couples. Merrick apologized each time, and then returned his gaze to watching his feet. Julia had never seen him blush before; now, his face was red like a fresh tomato. She felt sorry for him.

They made it through, and with only minor damage to Julia's toes. She was relieved when the song came to an end, and she could see in Merrick's face that whatever relief she felt, his was probably ten times greater.

"Thank you, Merrick," she said. "That was lovely."

He smiled for the first time in many minutes. "You're a poor liar," he said.

Sadly, this moment of connection was lost almost immediately. When they left the floor, Millie was there waiting for them, her eyes shiny with purpose.

"I was right. You two make such a handsome couple. Go again. Go on." She made shooing motions with her hands, trying to turn Julia and Merrick around.

"I'm a bit out of breath, Mrs. Jones," Julia said. "I think I'll take a break."

"Nonsense," Millie said, undeterred and most definitely immune to picking up on subtle social signals. "You're young! Get back out there and enjoy yourself." She grabbed Merrick by the elbow and once again tried to drag him toward Julia, but she might as well have tried dragging an oak through the forest by its branches.

When Julia glanced at Merrick, there was something akin to sorrow in his eyes. She briefly wondered if he was missing his wife. And so she tried to let him off the hook. Unfortunately her good intentions didn't make it all the way to her tongue. "Thank you for the dance, Constable Merrick. I'll let you go. I'm sure you have other things to attend to." As soon as the words were out of her mouth, she realized they sounded ungrateful and curt, and as though she didn't want to dance with him again. Which wasn't true.

Hurt flared briefly in the man's eyes, and then was gone and replaced by the cool, professional demeanor she so often saw in them. He made a small bob of his head, "As you wish, Miss Thom." He pulled his arm out of Millie's raptor grasp and walked away.

"Stupid, stupid woman." Julia wasn't sure if she was cursing herself or Mrs. Jones as she lifted her skirt and trudged down the front steps of the schoolhouse.

She reached the ground and spun on the heel of one buttoned boot to walk back the length of the building to the outhouse that was positioned several yards beyond the schoolhouse, among some young birch trees.

Night had landed with a thump. She hardly noticed the sparkly blanket of stars above her head as she strode along the path. The darkness was so absolute that her eyes might as well have been closed, although that didn't matter. She walked this path several times a day and did it without thinking. Her feet followed the route without instruction.

Millie Jones' interference tonight irritated Julia, but more than that she was angry at herself for hurting her new friend, Jack Merrick, albeit unintentionally. A small part of her recognized as well, though she was loathe to admit it, that Merrick affected her more than she was comfortable with.

Since she had arrived in Horse, her relationship with the tall and stoic police constable had been fraught with tension. She, with a quick mind and a judge for a father, had been denied her dream of attending law school. But this hadn't prevented her from getting embroiled in a little mystery involving one of her students a few weeks earlier. Constable Merrick had initially been reluctant to accept Julia's help, but eventually surrendered, as one does to the tide or the seasons. He recognized that fighting her would probably only cause him suffering. They'd reached a mutual detente and recently even seemed to be approaching something like an uneasy friendship. Now, though, she was afraid she'd destroyed whatever goodwill had been building between them.

She swung the outhouse door open and stepped inside, turning to latch it behind her. The chiding continued while she attended to her business, and then also as she closed the door behind her and began the walk back to the school. The music had started up again inside the building. It floated out of the open front door and swirled around her in the yard.

She was so wrapped up in her thoughts that she almost slammed into a man standing on the path. "Oh, excuse me," Julia said and stopped, expecting him to step to the side and leave the path to her.

"You're Miss Thom, aren't you?" the man said. The strong smell of whisky reached Julia's nose.

She took a better look at his face, his features murky in the dim-to-non-existent light. Without answering his question, she said, "Who are you?"

"Hear that, Bill?" the man said, with a mocking tone in his voice, "This little gem wants to know who we are."

Julia jumped slightly, suddenly realizing there was another man standing at her right elbow, so close she could hear him breathing. Even so, she refused to yield. "Excuse me," she said again, "I'd like to pass."

"Be my guest," the first man said, remaining stock still, standing on the path.

She couldn't step to her right because of the second man there. And she couldn't step to her left as the path at this point in its journey hugged tightly against a large maple tree before arching out again in a lazy curve. Julia wondered if these men had chosen this spot to wait for her deliberately. *Of course they did, idiot,* she chastised herself.

As any woman would do in this circumstance, Julia felt herself beginning to panic but worked hard to stay calm. She knew any sound she made would not be heard by anyone in the school; the building was still fifteen yards away. As well, the din of chatter, music and laughter had only increased as the evening progressed. Julia could scream herself hoarse and never be heard.

She could try to push through the men, though she expected that was exactly what they wanted. And the thought of touching either of them made her skin crawl.

So she did the only thing she could think of and took a quick step back and then tried to swiftly move around the second man. They had anticipated this, of course. Both men reached out as she moved and each grabbed one of her arms.

Julia froze and mustered her best school mistress voice. "Let me go."

The first man, clearly the leader of the team, laughed quietly and put his face right up to hers. He looked at her the way a cat looks at a mouse it has trapped. Squeezing her arm tightly he growled, "Not a chance now, Lassie. You're mine." He held up the glinting blade of a knife, the razor sharp kind you use to gut animals. With one finger he stroked the hair collected in a bun at the back of her neck.

His compatriot snorted and spat a wad of chewing tobacco onto the ground.

Julia pulled and struggled, trying to break free, but her arms were held fast.

The first man kept his lips close to Julia's cheek. "This'll teach you, teacher lady, to go out all by yerself." His breath smelled of the whisky she had noticed a moment ago, and also of something sour.

First Man pulled back slightly. Glancing quickly over his shoulder, he checked the path behind him and then jerked his head at his partner. "Quickly now," he said. And then to Julia, "If you make one sound I will cut that pretty face of yours all to pieces." He nodded once. "No foolin'."

Julia believed him.

Both men began to walk, pulling Julia with them, forcing her to walk backwards, toward the outhouse. They held her arms so tightly and moved so swiftly that they were basically carrying her. Julia glanced left and right hoping to see the flash of a match or some other sign that someone, anyone, was outside, but there was nothing. The men veered off the path and pulled Julia around the outhouse, into the cluster of trees at the very back of the school property.

The two men were utterly silent.

Julia tried kicking out at their legs, but they dodged the path of her flailing feet, and gripped her more tightly.

If she had thought it dark before, the darkness in the trees took things to another level. The lingering leaves blocked out any light from the stars and moon, and the shadows thrown by the tree trunks and branches were weighted with fear.

The journey into the trees took only seconds, though to Julia it seemed much longer than that.

The knife that First Man held continued to glimmer beside her throat despite the lack of light. The men, without saying anything to one another began to slow. They had chosen their spot.

Julia began to weigh the consequences of screaming and

was about to draw breath to do so when a voice came out of the night behind the men.

"Let her go."

Julia couldn't see anything. She ranged her head around wildly, but the dark mass of tree trunks was all that she could see.

The two men spun around, letting go of her arms. Julia was unprepared and fell to her knees.

Silence.

Second Man whispered, "Who's there?"

Julia rose from her knees and stumbled forward. First Man reached for her arm, trying to grab her again, when the voice came again, loud and sharp, "Do not do that."

First Man withdrew his hand as from a hot stove and Julia kept moving. She didn't recognize the voice but walked as quickly as she could toward it. A hand reached out. She saw the tiny flash of flesh in the velvet blackness. She reached and grabbed it; a drowning woman being pulled to shore.

The two men behind her must have recovered their wits and drunken bravado.

"I'll cut you down," First Man said and began moving to where Julia was standing.

The stranger's voice beside her came again. "Stay where you are."

First man made a scoffing noise, and kept moving, "Piss off."

A shot rang out, wild and eclipsing in the quiet. Julia jumped as though she'd been bitten. First Man howled and leapt back. His saucer eyes flashed like fireflies.

The voice beside Julia came again, "I said, leave her alone."

Both men froze. The air fairly crackled in the grove of trees.

"Go, Miss Thom. Go back to the dance."

Julia turned and finally recognized who was coming to her

aid. It was Mr. Hunter, the town clockmaker. He had a tiny silver pistol in his left hand. He took his eyes off the men for a second, "Go on."

Julia took a step sideways and then heard the whisper of leaves and scuffle of boots. The men disappeared, melting into the darkness. For a few moments, she and Mr. Hunter stood listening, and then the sounds were gone.

The clockmaker turned and offered Julia his elbow. "Let's go back inside."

CHAPTER TWO

The brouhaha that ensued when Hunter and Julia entered the school embarrassed her greatly. As Hunter guided her over the threshold, the adrenaline that had been surging through her body abandoned her all at once. She stumbled, righted herself, and then felt her knees buckle. Hunter wrapped his arm tightly around her waist and guided her to a chair near the door. Dancers turned. The chatter in the room magically evaporated like steam.

Betty Mitchell ran over to her friend. "Julia, are you okay? What's happened?"

Julia couldn't answer. Her throat wouldn't work. Nor would her composure. Betty knelt down beside the chair, and Julia's head collapsed onto her shoulder.

"I'll get her some water," Mr. Hunter said and disappeared.

The band stopped playing. Knots of people formed around Julia's chair. Merrick waded through them to get to her. Millie Jones, not to be outdone in the drama department, fainted, though she had no reason, as Julia hadn't said anything yet. She had to be fanned and consoled, and for this Julia was actually grateful. It took part of the spotlight off her.

Hunter returned to Julia's side with a glass of water.

Merrick turned to Hunter. "What happened?"

Hunter explained the part of the scene that he had wandered into. "I was walking by, out for my evening stroll, and I heard voices."

James Hunter was several inches taller than Julia and had dark, curly hair that looked perpetually messed on his head, as though someone had just ruffled it for him. He was clean-shaven, and smelled not unpleasantly of some sort of oil Julia assumed he used in his trade. His suit and vest were dark with a fine white pinstripe and, appropriately, the watch chain hanging across his mid-section looked substantial. Though the suit was well made, it seemed a size or two too large for the man. She wondered if he'd lost weight recently.

Julia looked at him, questioning, "You could hear me over all the music and noise from the dance?"

Hunter nodded. "I wasn't on Elm Street, out front. I was on Heather Street, in the back of the school. It was quite obvious while you were talking to those men that you were afraid."

When Hunter finished explaining, Merrick turned and scanned the faces of the crowd around him. He found Walt Sheehan standing a few feet away behind several onlookers. The constable jerked his head toward the front door. Walt pulled his banjo strap over his head and handed the instrument to Edgar Finnegan. He and Merrick disappeared into the darkness out the front door of the schoolhouse.

Julia looked up and found James Hunter standing a few feet away looking worried. To his left, the recovered Millie Jones sat on a chair, fanning herself and watching the scene, enraptured. On Hunter's right was Lily Cecil, a new employee at the Finnegan's hotel, whom Julia had only met once or twice. She had one hand on Hunter's arm. Beside and behind these three, the eyes of everyone else in the room were trained on Julia.

She took a few shuddering deep breaths and wiped her eyes with the handkerchief that appeared in her right hand. Her mind was having trouble grasping all that was happening and had happened. She felt herself shiver and when she looked to one side, noticed one of her students, Katherine Elias, kneeling on the floor beside her. Julia reached out and they held hands. Betty stayed crouched in front of Julia, providing a bit of a barrier from the others, for which Julia was grateful.

Merrick and Walt returned moments later, lanterns in hand. They set them on a table near the front door.

"Any sign of them?" Mayor Billy asked.

Merrick shook his head. "Did you recognize them?" he asked Julia.

She shook her head.

"What about you?" Merrick turned to Hunter who also responded in the negative.

Walt stayed back while Merrick stepped through the crowd to stand beside Julia. Katherine stepped out of the way. The constable crouched down, resting his backside on his heels. "Tell me as much as you remember about them," he said quietly. "Do you remember what they were wearing or any other details?"

Julia took a deep breath and sat up a little straighter. Merrick's face was below hers and it was a new experience to be looking down at him.

He continued, "Anything might be helpful, Julia. What accent did they have?"

It was a good question. Nearly everyone in Canada was very recently from somewhere else, or their parents were. Julia closed her eyes. "English," she said. "Not posh. Rough."

"Thick English?" Merrick asked, "As though they'd been raised there?"

"Yes."

"What else?"

"They smelled of whisky. At least the first one did. He's the one who got right up close to me." She shuddered.

"Good. That's good. Anything else?"

"One of them was chewing tobacco. Not the one with the knife. The other one." She cast her mind back, reluctantly closing her eyes. "The first one called the other one Bill. They were wearing long coats. Like stockmen. And they both had hats on. Black, I think." She was quiet for a few more seconds, searching her memory for clues. The room was silent, waiting. Finally she opened her eyes. "That's it. I don't remember any more."

"That's fine. You did well." Merrick stood up. "They could be drifters, or new drovers on a ranch. I'll have to ask around. We'll find them. Don't worry." He looked at Julia with concern, their mutual embarrassment about Millie Jones' matchmaking evaporating.

Merrick turned to Hunter and began asking him similar questions, but the clockmaker wasn't able to add much new information.

Though it was early, the dance was finished for that night. Heaped onto the residual fear Julia felt, was guilt at spoiling the event for the townspeople. She tried to protest when people began packing up their food, and gathering their coats, but Betty wouldn't hear her protestations.

"It's not your fault, Julia. We are your friends. We want to help."

Betty helped Julia gather her shawl and bag.

As she began to leave the building with Betty and her husband, Christopher, a thought suddenly occurred to her. She turned and found Merrick standing close by, conferring with Mayor Billy, Walt and Edgar Finnegan. "They knew who I was."

Merrick's eyebrows drew closer together. "Really?"

"Yes, they called me by name."

CHAPTER THREE

Elise Campbell had fallen and torn her stockings. Grit and small bits of gravel were ground into the soft skin on her knee. The girl sniffled as Julia wiped blood carefully away and dabbed the wound with a soft cloth.

This was one aspect of the job of schoolteacher that Julia had not been prepared for; she was mother hen during the day to all the children who filled the schoolhouse. Raised as an only child, she was unprepared for the maternal feelings that were growing within her with each passing day. Elise was just the latest in a string of injuries that had befallen the pupils on that Monday. Julia wasn't sure if it was because she was rattled from the events of the dance two nights previous, but there seemed to be some sort of curse on the classroom. Edgar Butters tripped first thing in the morning and banged his head on the side of Julia's desk. Luckily the boy's skull appeared to be impervious to ill treatment, and he was laughing about it with the other boys in the yard at lunch. A bird flew into one of the windows and landed with a soft thud in the yard. That accident had turned into a science lesson. Julia found a basket and laid an old tea towel in the bottom. She and the students all trooped outside and gathered the bird up, bringing it inside, away from predators. It was a purple finch, which brought on discussions of migration and eating habits, which Julia much preferred to rote teaching of the multiplication tables.

But the catastrophes weren't over yet. After lunch the two youngest pupils got into a spat, the genesis of which Julia was still not sure she understood. They had to be separated, which caused them both to sulk for the remainder of the day. And then, just as Julia was locking up the doors to go home, Elise came up the schoolhouse stairs, weeping with her bloody knee on display.

"There," Julia said, giving the knee a final swipe with her cloth, "it's all clean. Feel better?" She looked up from where she was kneeling in front of Elise. The child was shuddering softly with the leftover breaths of weeping. She had the end of one of her braids in her mouth. Julia reached up and removed it. "Come on," she said, "I'll walk you home."

The girl's dark eyes brightened at this. She wiped her nose on her sleeve.

THE DAY BEFORE, Sunday, Julia had woken in an unfamiliar bed. It took her a few moments to realize she was in the Mitchells' spare bedroom. They had coddled her; making her a lovely breakfast of fresh boiled eggs, thick slices of bacon and fresh baked scones. Together they walked to church and bumped into Merrick on their way.

Merrick and Julia fell into step a few houses down from the school that would be operating as the church. Merrick was wearing what Julia had come to recognize as his Sunday suit. He had on the black, wide-brimmed hat he always wore. Julia had never seen Merrick look untidy and today was no exception. He was clean-shaven, and the silver watch-chain on his vest gleamed. Some men look ill-suited to their profession; the thin cook or the sickly doctor. Merrick was not one of these.

He was tall and imposing, and when at rest his expression was often solemn. Julia knew him to be kind and fair, but criminals would not make that assumption at first glance. He knew how to use his height and stature to his advantage. Now his blue-green eyes looked at her cautiously.

"How are you?" the constable asked.

"Fine, thank you. And thank you for last night."

"I did nothing. Mr. Hunter deserves all the credit."

"I am so grateful to him. But also to you. And everyone." She glanced back briefly at the Mitchells, who walked arm-in-arm.

Merrick looked down at her. "Today I'm going to ride out to Middle Lake Ranch and talk to Herbert Green. He's got several new drovers, I think, and I want to talk to them."

Julia thought about this for a minute. "I should go with you."

Merrick stopped in his tracks, and stared at her. "You must be joking."

"No, I'm not. You need to identify the men, and Mr. Hunter and I are the only people who can do that."

The Mitchells caught up to them and Merrick's feet began to move forward again by rote. "Don't be ridiculous. I'll ask at the ranch, and if anyone acts suspicious or doesn't have a good explanation for where they were last night, I'll bring them in. You can identify them then, if necessary."

Merrick seemed to be waiting for her to protest but when she didn't he nodded gently to himself.

She wouldn't confess as much to Merrick, but she was relieved he had turned down her idea. After church she wanted to spend the rest of the day making herself a bath and then soaking in it for as long as the water stayed warm.

ELISE DIDN'T SPEAK while they walked down the street toward her home, but she held Julia's hand as she limped. Julia was quiet, also. Her bath the day before had been just what the doctor ordered, and the Mitchells had insisted she join them again that night for their Sunday roast dinner. They invited her to sleep there again, but she declined this time, wanting to get back to a routine that felt normal. Hoping that by doing so, she would begin to feel less shattered and anxious.

Julia and her pupil arrived at Elise's front door. Elise pushed it open and called out, "Mother?"

Mrs. Campbell appeared from the kitchen. The house smelled pleasantly of cooked onions and fresh bread.

Elise began to cry again when she saw her mother.

"Oh, my darlin'. What's happened?"

"She's fine, Mrs. Campbell," Julia assured her from the threshold. "Just a little scrape."

Beth Campbell crouched down and used the tea towel in her hand to wipe the tears from her daughter's face. She murmured softly to the girl for a few moments.

"Go on, now," she said, standing up, "Go take those stockings off and put on your after school dress. Bring me your stockings once you've got them off and I'll darn them." She kissed the girl's cheek.

When Elise was gone, Beth stood.

"Let me make you a cup of tea, Miss Thom."

"I'd better not, Mrs. Campbell. I want to get to the clock shop before it closes. I want to thank Mr. Hunter for his help the other night." Hunter had not been at church the day before, and Julia couldn't remember if she'd thanked him sufficiently on Saturday night.

Beth nodded and then the light in her eyes shifted slightly. "I was so sorry to hear about what happened to you at the dance, Miss Thom. That must have been awfully frightening."

"It was a little unsettling, I must say," Julia conceded. The truth was that she had been more rattled by the event than she cared to admit. She had hardly slept at the Mitchells, and then in her own bed Sunday night, and felt herself anxiously looking over her shoulder several times during the day at school. She couldn't get the smell of the two men - a mixture of chewing tobacco, whisky and sweat - out of her nose.

"How nice that Mr. Hunter was there for you. He's such a lovely man. Quiet." She stopped, her eyes glancing down, thinking. "I don't actually know if I've heard the man say more than three words. But there are worse qualities in a man, aren't there?"

Julia smiled, and shifted uncomfortably where she stood, now waiting for the first opportunity to leave the house.

"He certainly came to your aid. A gun! My goodness." Beth clutched her hands to her chest, enjoying the drama.

"It was just a tiny little thing," Julia said, wondering why she was downplaying the size of the gun.

"The bullets still come out of it just as quickly as a large gun, I'm sure." Beth laughed a tinkly little twitter and Julia had to smile as well.

"I must be going, Mrs. Campbell," Julia said and backed toward the door. "I just wanted to see Elise safely delivered."

"Of course, Miss Thom. Thank you." Beth moved forward and just before Julia made her escape she put a hand on the teacher's arm. "You must tell me if Mr. Hunter refers to the escapades from Saturday night when you see him this afternoon. He must be feeling quite gallant."

JULIA CURSED under her breath as she reacted to what seemed to be the collective town project that looked to involve marrying her off. She'd left her family home for just such a reason. Her parents didn't want her educated, they wanted her married. Despite encouraging her intelligence when she was a child, when push came to shove all her parents wanted from her were grandchildren. Julia's father had been her best friend, teaching her all he knew about the law. But when she began talking in earnest of applying to law school, even though no woman had yet attended one in Canada, he balked. Words were flung. Tears were cried. Julia felt betrayed by the man who, for the whole of her life thus far, has been her greatest ally. She had come to Horse in a rash move to punish her father, but also to escape the preordained role as wife and mother that she had felt herself being pushed into. *And now I find myself in the same damn predicament*, she thought as she stomped down the street. *People being shoved in my face at dances, and matches made with men who inexplicably carry guns.*

She turned onto Main Street, her thoughts swirling, her anger growing and bouncing around inside her like a rubber ball in a drum. She wasn't quite ready to admit to herself that it felt better to be angry than to reflect on how afraid she'd been the night of the dance. As she walked down the wooden sidewalk, her heels tapping, she thought about what Mr. Hunter had done for her. She was grateful. About that there was no doubt. But she was not attracted to the man. Was she?

Julia came to a stop on the sidewalk. Now she was second-guessing herself. Mr. Hunter was an attractive man in an unshowy kind of way. Did she have feelings for him?

She shook her head and scoffed at herself. The townsfolk had gotten inside her head. Especially that passive-aggressive Millie Jones who would like nothing more than to have Julia married off to the first man who had laid eyes on her. She resumed her steps and hopped down off the end of the side-walk when she reached Third Avenue.

Mr. Hunter's shop was three doors past the corner. In the front window sat a display on an old pine dresser with several pocket watches and a mantel clock.

The door creaked as it opened, and Julia closed it firmly behind her. She was determined to be as professional and courteous as possible, but she was not going to let others' ideas about her and Mr. Hunter cloud her mind.

The shop rustled with the ticking of many clocks. There were several small wall clocks in the front of the shop, their pendulums swinging. Julia feigned interest in them for a moment, while she waited for Mr. Hunter to attend to her. A small counter stretched across the middle of the store, dividing the shop into front and back. Behind the counter was a wall and a doorway, and beyond that Mr. Hunter's workspace. Julia could see a workbench, crowded with tools and also the innards of what she assumed was a watch, laid out on what looked like a piece of dark velvet. She listened for a moment, trying to detect sounds coming from the workshop, but there were none. Perhaps Mr. Hunter was out back at the privy.

She waited.

After a few more moments with no sign of the proprietor, Julia went to the counter and called through the doorway behind it, "Hello? Mr. Hunter?"

She waited, ears perked.

Perhaps he had been called away. It seemed strange that he'd leave the door open in that case, but perhaps it was an emergency.

Julia shrugged, relieved in a way not to have to face Mr. Hunter while she was still riled up. She turned and walked to the front door and yanked it open, perhaps slightly more aggressively than entirely necessary.

Just as she raised her foot to step across the threshold she heard something. Turning, she waited. There it was again. At first she thought it was one of the clocks making an odd noise. But then it came again and she recognized it for what it was. A groan.

She let go of the door and turned back. "Mr. Hunter?" she asked again, this time with fear touching her voice.

At the far left of the counter was a gap with a small, knee-to-waist-height swinging door. Julia, still listening, walked to it and pushed through, aiming to go to the workspace in the back of the shop. But she was brought up short. There, on the floor behind the counter, lay Mr. Hunter. One of his arms was crumpled under him at an odd angle. He was lying on his stomach. There was a tear in one sleeve of his white shirt and his dark suit trousers looked splattered with some kind of dark liquid. His head was turned and rested on one cheek and the side facing Julia was covered in blood. The right eye was swollen almost completely shut; it bulged out from Hunter's face like a small balloon.

Julia dropped to her knees and fumbled in her handbag for a handkerchief. "Oh dear, oh dear. Mr. Hunter, can you hear me?"

She flung her purse to one side when she realized her handkerchief was not there. She must have left it at the school after using it to minister to Elise. Julia leaned forward and touched the man's arm gently. "Mr. Hunter? Are you awake? Can you hear me?"

Something was digging into her left knee. She shifted slightly, and reached down with one gloved hand to brush away whatever it was. As her hand touched the offending object she caught a glimpse of it before it shot away from her touch and bounced off the baseboard behind her. It was a tooth.

CHAPTER FOUR

"Can you hold up your side a bit better please?"

"I'm trying but you've got him hoisted so far up on your side that his weight is sliding down on me. You're both taller than me, you know," Julia said crossly, and slightly out of breath.

"Okay, stop then. Let's try something else." Merrick stopped walking and shifted Hunter so that his arm wasn't around Merrick's shoulder. "Is that better?"

"Yes." Julia said.

They kept walking.

HUNTER NEEDED MEDICAL ATTENTION, that much was obvious. Julia debated for a few seconds about running all the way through town to Dr. Parker's office to get him and bring him back to the store. She ran out into the street and, as luck would have it, Constable Merrick was riding by. He took one look at Julia's face and leapt off Earl, his big grey. He quickly threw the reins over the closest hitching post and followed Julia without a word into Hunter's store. After a quick assessment, Merrick decided it would be better to just take Hunter to the doctor's office.

"Stay here. I'll go get Walt."

"Don't be ridiculous," Julia said, refusing to be relegated to the status of frail bystander. "We shouldn't waste time. Let's get him up into sitting position."

When they did, the situation briefly worsened. Hunter's vest and shirt front were liberally covered in blood. His nose was sitting at an odd angle and was nearly as swollen as his right eye. His left eye still remained slightly open, but Julia expected that situation wouldn't last long. The right arm was clearly broken. Hunter moaned loudly when they sat him up.

From there, as gently as they could, Julia and Merrick got Hunter standing between them. He was conscious, but just barely, and his feet dragged occasionally as they pulled/carried him out of the shop.

Dr. Parker was waiting for them when they reached his surgery. Christopher Mitchell had been coming back from a delivery and spotted the ragged trio inching their way along Main Street. He'd run to the doctor to prepare him.

"Put him on the table. Gently now."

Julia and Merrick slowly made their way down the hallway at the front of Parker's house. In his office, the examination table was covered with a fresh sheet and lying flat.

Julia and Merrick leaned Hunter against the table at its middle. Merrick unwound his arm from Hunter's side and then while Julia squiggled out of the way, the doctor and Merrick gently lifted the patient up onto the bed. Hunter groaned once and his head flopped back dramatically as he fainted for the first time since they'd left the store.

"What happened?" Parker leaned over Hunter's face as Merrick stepped out of the way.

"I don't know," Julia answered. "I found him like this behind the counter at his store."

Merrick turned to Julia. "Did you see anyone around the shop when you arrived?"

Julia shook her head. Now that Hunter was safely in the doctor's care, the adrenaline was leaving her body. She cleared her throat, "No. There was no one. The shop was quiet. I almost left because I thought he wasn't there."

Parker turned away from the examining table and walked to a cabinet filled with glass jars that held various sharp and dangerous-looking instruments. He grabbed a pair of scissors and two towels off a pile on a lower shelf.

"Did you see any horses around when you arrived?" Merrick continued questioning Julia. "Any wagons hitched nearby?"

Julia cast her mind back to the scene on the street. She had been so preoccupied with angry thoughts about her status as a project in the minds of the town's matchmakers that she doubted she would have noticed a stagecoach even if it had run over her. She shook her head.

Dr. Parker undid the buttons on Hunter's vest and pushed it aside. The shirt underneath was still white in the places where the vest had protected it. Parker leaned across with his scissors and began cutting away the shirt from around the broken arm.

Suddenly Hunter lifted his head off the bed. He groaned and began struggling, trying to sit up, although without much steam behind the attempt. Merrick moved a step closer to assist, but Parker was able to calm the man with a few words. He placed both hands on Hunter's shoulders and eased him back down.

Hunter said something that Julia didn't catch, and Dr. Parker had to lean in and turn his head to place his ear close to Hunter's mouth. Things were quiet for a moment and then the doctor straightened up and turned to Merrick, "I think you can leave us now. He'll be fine with me. I'll set this arm and look after his cuts and bruises." He turned to Julia. "Miss Thom, could you find Eleanor, please, and send her? She's probably at the Mitchell's store."

Julia nodded and Merrick followed her out of the room and then out of the house.

CHAPTER FIVE

B etty Mitchell ladled a generous portion of stew from the large Dutch oven into a smaller pot that Julia held out for her. The stew smelled richly of onion and roasted venison. It made Julia's mouth water.

When the smaller pot was full, Julia waited while Betty wrapped up two loaves of bread and six scones. They were heading over to James Hunter's house to check in on him and make sure he was eating.

Betty was Julia's closest friend in Horse. On the surface they had very little in common; Betty was married and had come to British Columbia from Canada's far eastern maritime provinces. She and her ridiculously handsome husband, Christopher, owned and ran the General Store. They were childless, which brought tears to Betty's eyes every time it was mentioned in Julia's presence. The couple poured their love and attention into their shop and it showed. It was the loveliest little store for hundreds of miles and the Mitchell's were justifiably proud of what they'd built. Betty and Julia had bonded initially out of necessity, perhaps. The ratio of men to women in a place this remote was overwhelming. Secretly, Betty wanted to keep an eye on Julia; to keep her safe from the possibly predatory men who might want to hitch their wagons, and their kitchens, to Julia. She needn't have worried. Julia was far too enamored of her new status as a single working woman to throw it away for some man with a quarter section and most of his own hair.

Betty kissed her husband goodbye, which made Julia avert her eyes, and the two women proceeded down Main Street toward Hunter's little house that was tucked away in the street just behind his shop.

Doctor Parker had set Hunter's arm in a splint. He said the break wasn't too bad and that Hunter should regain the use of the arm in no time. Julia assumed this was a huge relief to Hunter. A watchmaker with only one working arm was like a clock with just one hand.

"Yoo hoo! Mr. Hunter!" Betty called as she tapped gently on the front door and then opened it without waiting. Julia loved her friend's implacable friendliness. It was totally without guile and one of Julia's favorite things about Mrs. Mitchell. It would never occur to Betty that someone might not appreciate her barging into their home. In her mind, she was there on a mission of goodwill and closed doors didn't mean much to her in that case.

"Hello?" the querying voice came from the back of the house, unsure of itself.

"Mr. Hunter, it's Betty Mitchell and Julia Thom. We're here with provisions. May we come in?" Betty was already standing in the front hall, eyeing the kitchen.

There was some rustling and a thump from the bedroom and then Hunter appeared in the doorway, clad in a striped dressing gown over what appeared to be a long nightshirt. His hair was rumpled from his pillow and he held the splinted arm gingerly with the other.

"Um..." he said, looking confused.

"Don't fight it, Mr. Hunter," Julia said, smiling at him. "You'll not win. We won't stay long. We just brought you some bread and scones, and some of Christopher Mitchell's famous venison stew."

"I ...uh..." the man blinked several times but was at a loss for words.

"We'll just put these things in the kitchen, shall we?" Betty marched off into the small kitchen, and Julia followed in her wake.

For the next hour Betty bustled about, lighting the stove to keep the stew warm, tidying and washing the dirty dishes, and generally making herself very much at home. Julia soon realized that she would only be in the way, so she asked Mr. Hunter to join her in the living room where they could chat.

The swelling had gone down around Hunter's eyes, and they had reopened slightly. His face was several different shades of blue and purple. There was a cut on his lower lip that Julia hadn't noticed when she'd been helping him. His nose, which had been the source of most of the blood at the scene, was swollen as well, and from where Julia sat, it also looked slightly crooked now. Although she thought that could just be an illusion of the swelling.

She got Hunter settled on the sofa, putting a pillow in his lap to rest his broken arm on. She took the blanket off his bed and put it over his legs.

"I'm not an old woman," he said, protesting slightly.

"I know, but let me fuss," Julia said. "You helped me the other night. Let me return the favor."

Julia's first meeting with Hunter had been a week earlier. He had come to her house to repair her grandmother clock, one of the few possessions other than clothes that she had brought with her from her family home. At the time, while she had watched him work, she had experienced him as a man who was reserved to the point of near-muteness. He was polite with her, and very competent at his job - he had the clock fixed very quickly with seemingly no difficulty at all - but he seemed decidedly uncomfortable in her presence.

When they were settled, Julia looked around the room, which was much like her own little living room; it had a small parlor stove in one corner, a bookcase against a wall, the upholstered chair she was sitting in and the two-seater sofa where Hunter rested. The furniture looked well taken care of, though not new. And around the room Julia saw several clocks, mounted on the walls, all ticking gently.

"You'll never be late for anything will you, Mr. Hunter?" she teased him.

"Hazard of the trade, I'm afraid," he said, "Every once in a while someone wants to sell a real beauty. They make a good investment so I buy them, and then I can't seem to bring myself to sell them." He shrugged, obviously willing to accept his own weaknesses.

Just for something to say, Julia asked about the history of the clocks. Hunter spent a very content fifteen minutes telling her where each one had come from, its pedigree, and its manufacturer. Even some background on each manufacturer and where they stood now in the world of clock making.

He glanced at Julia after a story about pendulums and stopped mid-sentence. "I'm boring you."

"Not at all," Julia lied, "I had no idea the world of clocks had so much intrigue."

There was a pause and Julia listened to the clatter of dishes and crockery in the kitchen. She and Mr. Hunter smiled at each other in a shared moment of chagrin about getting in Betty Mitchell's way.

Finally Hunter said, "How are you feeling after your...encounter on Saturday evening?"

Julia shifted in her chair, remembering her fright on that night, and Mr. Hunter's gallantry.

"I'm sorry," the man said, noticing Julia's discomfort. "I didn't mean to upset you all over again."

"No, it's no trouble. I just hadn't thought about it for awhile what with..." she gestured toward Hunter himself.

Hunter grimaced. "I'm so sorry you had to see that."

"Please, don't, Mr. Hunter. I am so happy I came into your shop when I did. I hate to think what would have happened if I hadn't."

"As do I. Your timing was impeccable." Hunter paused, thinking. "Did Dr. Parker come to the shop and take me to the surgery?"

"Don't you remember?"

Hunter shook his head.

"Well, no," Julia explained, "Constable Merrick and I walked you to his office." Now it was Julia's turn to ask a question, "Do you know who it was that attacked you?"

Reflexively Hunter reached up and touched his nose and then pulled his hand away quickly. "I really don't remember very much."

"Do you think it was the two men who were..." Julia wasn't sure what word to use, "being so rude to me on the night of the dance?"

"I don't know, Miss Thom. I really can't say. The men at the dance were almost impossible for me to see, with the darkness and the shadows from the trees. Can you remember what they looked like?"

Julia shook her head. "I just have a vague impression. It's their voices I remember most. Did your attacker or attackers speak to you?"

Hunter hesitated slightly, thinking, "My memory of the event is quite muddled. I really can't remember much at all."

"Did they steal anything?"

The clockmaker had been looking away in the middle distance, perhaps remembering the beating. He brought his eyes back to Julia now. "Anything from the shop?" he asked, seeming puzzled and then recovering. "Oh. I see what you're asking. Well, no, I don't think so. But to be honest I haven't been back there since Dr. Parker brought me home last night."

"I'm sure Constable Merrick will ask you this, if he hasn't

already. But I must ask: do you have any idea why you were attacked?"

Hunter seemed to be growing increasingly uncomfortable. He gently raised his broken arm and shifted the pillow in his lap. Even taking into consideration the bruising around his eyes, he looked frightfully exhausted. Julia wondered if he'd slept at all. It couldn't be easy with the arm the way it was.

Julia stood up, feeling she'd been insensitive to Mr. Hunter's discomfort. "Do you have any whisky?" she asked.

Hunter looked at her with a furrowed brow. "It's not yet noon, Miss Thom."

"Never mind that. You're obviously in considerable pain."

Hunter pointed to a short, narrow cabinet that stood in a corner of the room. In it Julia found a small bottle of whisky. There were no glasses present so she went to the kitchen to find one. Betty had found an apron and tied it around her waist. She was stirring the stew and had placed thick slices of her bread on the kitchen table on a plate. The butter dish was standing at the ready, as was a bowl for stew. "You can ask Mr. Hunter to sit up at the table, Julia. It's time to get some food in him."

Julia took a short glass, which was delicately etched with a leaf and vine motif, off one of the shelves and took it back in the living room. She poured a measure and waited while Hunter drank it.

"Betty says lunch is ready," she said when Hunter handed her the glass back.

"I confess I'm not all that hungry."

Julia returned the whisky bottle to its cabinet and turned to face the patient. "I'm not sure that's going to matter to Mrs. Mitchell," she said, grinning.

~

THE WATCH MAKER'S shop was exactly as Merrick and Julia had left it the day before. Julia could even see drops of blood on the floor behind the counter.

Hunter had been falling asleep in his stew when Betty showed some mercy and let him leave the table without finishing. She took him to his room, propriety be damned, and tucked him into his single bed, his arm resting beside him on the pillow he'd been using in the living room. Something Dr. Parker had not thought to do the night before.

"Men!" Betty scoffed when she returned to the kitchen to help Julia wrap up the bread and scones. "Dr. Parker is an excellent physician but as a nurse he is sorely lacking. Leaving that man in his bed without any relief for his arm. It's such a simple thing to do. That pillow makes all the difference to him. He's asleep already." Betty fussed and muttered, her maternal instincts getting a rare opportunity to be in full sail.

The ladies left a small fire going in the stove, and the pot of what stew remained on top, so that Hunter could have more when he awoke. They had promised Hunter they would look in on the shop.

The front was tidy, as it had been when Julia had been there the day before. It was in the back, the workshop area, where the evidence of the battle that had occurred lay.

Hunter had told them that he had a vague impression that whoever had attacked him had come in through the back door that led out onto the laneway that ran behind this row of shops on Main Street. Hunter had no real use for the lane, as his deliveries were small and periodic. Unlike the Mitchells, who had a small paddock for their horse and a parking spot for the delivery wagon, the back of Hunter's shop was simply a bare patch of dirt with a dry watering trough set to one side and an outhouse. Julia and Betty glanced at it briefly and then went back inside.

The workshop bore the evidence of the melee. Gears and rods and springs were scattered all over the floor like cherry blossom petals in spring. The two women tip-toed around them, trying not to crush anything under their buttoned boots. They spent twenty minutes carefully picking up every piece of hardware and every tool they could find.

A second table, separate from the one where Hunter appeared to do most of his work, had been knocked over, and this seemed to be the source of most of the confettied clock pieces. Julia and Betty lifted it back into position against the wall that bordered the front of the shop and put the clock pieces on it.

Lining the walls of the workshop were shelves that reached almost to the ceiling. These were filled with small and larger clocks, either awaiting repair or perhaps awaiting pick-up by their owners. Smaller shelves over Hunter's workbench held pocket watches, also in wait of repair or cleaning. Each one had a small tag attached to it with a string, usually tied around the chain, with the owner's name written in a neat and precise script. Julia saw Walt Sheehan's name on one of the watches. Its face was liberally scratched but when she picked it up and turned it over she saw that it had a beautiful Celtic cross carved into the back.

"Look at this," Betty said from behind her.

Julia put the watch back where it had been, and joined Betty by the back door. Her friend was standing over a third, narrow table that stood under the widow on the back wall of the shop. The window overlooked the lane and provided what Julia assumed was much-needed light in the space. The three tables in the workshop were separate but they formed a U-shape in the room, leaving space in the middle for Hunter's chair. The table Betty stood beside was only eight inches deep and had two hand-made wooden trays lying side-by-side on it. The trays were divided into smaller compartments and each compartment seemed to have a specific type of gear, spring or mechanical object in it. Julia looked at the trays, not under-standing what Betty wanted her to see.

"No, here." Betty pointed to the floor below the table. There was a single work glove lying on its back, fingers slightly curled.

Julia bent down and picked it up. It was leather and well-worn. There was a hole beginning to form in the index finger, and the entire thing seemed covered in layers of stains. Julia imagined it had been the light tan of deerskin originally.

Together both women scanned the shop for the glove's mate, but the only other piece of clothing they saw was Hunter's apron, which was hanging on a hook affixed to the wall between his primary workbench and the doorway to the front of the shop.

"That doesn't look like a watchmaker's glove to me," Betty said.

Julia turned it over in her hands. "Look at the size of it. Hunter's hands are not even close to being this big. They're delicate. Perfect for a watchmaker."

The two women raised their heads in concert and looked at one another. "It was dropped by whoever assaulted Hunter," Betty said.

Light came into Julia's eyes and she smiled. "It's a clue."

CHAPTER SIX

"Merrick won't thank you for interfering, Julia Thom," Betty said as they walked back from Hunter's shop toward Merrick's office, but she had a big smile on her face. Watching her new friend torment the normally kind and even-tempered constable with her meddling had become a great source of amusement for Betty. She was not a natural meddler herself, but she had no problem watching Julia get involved where she shouldn't.

"I'm not interfering," Julia countered, though she knew full-well this wasn't true. "I'm helping."

But Merrick wasn't in his office. The door was closed and when Julia marched in anyway the room was quiet and the stove cold.

So the two friends carried on down the street and when Betty returned to her store, she winked at Julia and said, "Promise me you'll tell me what expletive Merrick uses when he sees you."

"Oh, pffft," was the only retort Julia could come up with at the time.

The rhythmic clang-clang of Walter Sheehan's hammer meeting its target found Julia's ears long before she reached the blacksmith shop. She wondered briefly what it was like for Walt knowing that everyone in town knew where he was by following that noise. He was a quiet man, only given to speaking when he had something to say. And like most quiet people, he was keenly observant. Though Julia had only known him a few weeks, she could already tell that very little slipped past Walt. In this way, he was invaluable to his friend, Constable Jack Merrick.

Julia walked past the sleeping forms of the three dogs that were never far from Walt's side. The blacksmith nodded to Julia when she entered the shop but kept hammering for a moment. The nail he was forming was still red from the fire. Julia glanced around but Merrick was not in the blacksmith shop.

"One moment, lass," he said.

Originally and recently from Ireland, Walt was the only man in town who topped Merrick's height. The two men looked like Grecian pillars when they stood beside one another. But unlike his friend, Walt had the fair skin and fine, light brown hair of the Celts. His hands were always dirty; his profession did not allow him to ever be clean for long. His expression was usually serious, but when he looked at Julia, a long dormant warmth formed in his eyes. His nose was slightly too big for his face, but he was handsome in his own rugged way. There were small lines beside his clear blue eyes that Julia found charming. Though he rarely referred to his past, Julia got the impression he'd left Ireland under some sort of cloud. Twice since she'd arrived in August, Julia had had a chance to observe this natural observer when he didn't realize he was being watched. Both times, she'd seen a sorrow in his expression that nearly took her breath away.

Today though, the big Irishman was all smiles. Julia waited while Walt put the finishing touches on the nail, dunked it into the bucket of water beside him, and then tossed it onto a pile of nearly identical nails in a basket at his feet. He came around the anvil, hammer still in hand.

"What've you got there?" He nodded his head toward the glove. It would have taken much more time for any other man to notice she was carrying it. Walt the Observer.

"I found it at James Hunter's shop."

"Aye?" Walt reached for it, "May I?"

"Of course."

He set his hammer down on the chair by the front door and took the glove in his own hands, his blackened fingers holding it gently despite their size and strength. After running his eyes and fingers over it, and turning it over twice he handed it back to Julia.

"What are you thinking?" he asked.

"We found it by itself."

"Who's 'we'?"

"Betty Mitchell and I."

Walt nodded. "Go on."

"We found it by itself in Hunter's shop and I'm convinced it's not his."

"You'd be right about that. Look at the size of it. Hunter is a wee little thing. I could snap him in half and cook him for breakfast." He grinned at Julia. "And I'd still be hungry."

She smiled. No doubt Walt was right. "It looks like a ranch hand's glove to me. What do you think? See there, where it's been worn in a line?" She pointed to a darkened stripe that ran across the palm of the glove.

"Reins," Walt said simply.

Julia nodded, "Exactly."

"Well," Walt took in a deep breath and stood up straighter. He put his closed fists on his hips and arched into them. "You'd best go talk to the Major-General," he said, meaning Merrick. "He'll be wanting to know who set the boots to Hunter."

"He's not at his office. Do you know where he is?"

Walt jerked his head to his left, indicating the building next door, which was the other half of his business, the town livery. "Earl's got a bit o' a cough so he's ministering to him. Babying him, more like." But he smiled as he said it. Animals were one weakness of Walt's that Julia had noticed. He was friend to every dog and horse in town. Even the backyard chickens loved him. The three dogs of unknown origin who hung around the blacksmith shop and livery all day were no exception. They watched Walt's every move with the adoration of apostles.

"Thanks." Julia turned to leave the darkness and heat of the forge.

Walt picked his hammer up off the chair. "When he starts yelling I'll come and rescue you."

"Rescue him, you mean," Julia said, smiling.

BIG MEN NEED BIG HORSES, and Merrick's grey gelding was no exception. Earl was, at minimum, seventeen hands high and had feathered feet that were larger than Julia's head. Like Merrick, he was intimidating to look at but as gentle as a kitten when you got to know him. Merrick and his horse were a matched pair; both strong, steady, with even tempers and endless stamina. Earl was a little quicker to display affection, however.

When Julia poked her head over the half-door and greeted the constable and his ailing animal, Earl gently pushed Merrick out of the way and stepped over to greet her. He lifted his head over the door so Julia could rub his nose and cheek and whisper sweet nothings to him.

Merrick let this go on for a few moments and then asked, "Are you two about done?"

Julia grabbed a carrot out of the basket at the front of the livery. She broke it in half and held one piece of it out to Earl on her flattened palm. The crunching noises that issued from the big grey's mouth sent a frisson of pleasure through Julia.

Julia's own horse, Stanley, a paint horse with intelligent eyes and a curiosity that was never satisfied, just like his owner, poked his head out from his stall as well. His mistress walked down the center aisle of the barn and gave Stanley the other half of the carrot. With both horses happily munching, Merrick came out of Earl's stall.

He was wearing his usual dark suit, although at the moment his jacket was off and hanging from a hook on a post nearby. He had rolled up the sleeves of his shirt and was putting the lid back on a tin of ointment that smelled strongly of menthol. His vest was a little scrunched up and his hands looked a shiny from the ointment. Merrick glowered at Julia briefly, but she didn't take it personally. She had the sense she ruffled his feathers somewhat. He turned and walked all the way down the aisle to the tack room and disappeared inside. When he reemerged seconds later he was rubbing his hands on an old piece of cloth, removing the greasy liniment.

"Is Earl okay?" Julia asked.

"He'll be fine. He's just got a bit of a cough. It's almost gone." Like most men, Earl was probably loathe to admit he needed any special care. He withdrew his head back into the stall when he recognized Julia was out of carrots.

Julia came right to the point. "I found something." She held the glove out to Merrick.

The constable draped the cloth over the top rail of an empty stall and took the glove from her. He was quiet, turning it over just as Walt had done. Then he looked up at Julia, a hint of amusement in his eyes, "It's a glove."

She smiled. "Thank you for that."

"What's significant about this?"

"I found it at James Hunter's shop."

"And it's not his." This was a statement, not a question. "Just the one?"

Julia nodded. "I think it could belong to the man or men that attacked him."

Merrick handed the glove back to her. "Perhaps."

Julia's brows came together in a look of concern. "Are you going to look into it?"

"No," Merrick began unrolling his sleeves and buttoning them at the cuff. "It could have been dropped by anyone."

"But look," Julia pointed to the glove's palm, "Walt and I think that's the mark a reign makes. Whoever's glove this is works with horses. It could belong to one of the drovers from around here."

Merrick stood frozen while working at one cuff button. "'Walt and I'?" he asked.

Julia looked at him defiantly. She stood up a little straighter. "Yes. Walt and I discussed the glove just now. I found him next door before I knew you were here."

"Huh," Merrick began rolling his other sleeve down, "Well then, I will leave it to you and Walt to figure out who the glove belongs to."

"Good heavens, Constable Merrick, what's gotten up your nose this morning? I didn't think you'd be so petulant."

"Not petulant, Miss Thom, just busy. I've got paperwork on my desk that's about to swamp me, brands to check on several different ranches, and just for fun I thought I might have a stab at trying to find out who attempted to attack you the other night. If that's all right with you. So if you don't mind, I'll go take care of some of those things and leave you and Mr. Sheehan to discover just who the rightful owner of this glove is."

Julia's back was up now. She felt as though Merrick was attacking her for no good reason. "What about James Hunter? Isn't it also your responsibility to find out who attacked him? What if whoever it was comes after someone else in the community?"

Merrick pulled his jacket off the hook with a sharp jerk,

"Not that it's any of your business, but Mr. Hunter is not cooperating. I've spoken to him twice so far today and he won't answer any of my questions. Swears he's got amniotic something-or-other."

Julia stifled a smile, "I think you mean amnesia."

"Whatever. The point is he won't cooperate so there's not much else I can do. Without a witness or, heaven forbid, any details about what happened, my hands are tied. Now, if you'll excuse me."

Julia stepped aside to let Merrick pass. The constable sailed down the aisle and went out into the light outside without looking back. Julia turned and looked at Earl, who stood with his eyelids half-closed. "He's not an easy one to manage, is he?"

CHAPTER SEVEN

Through the large front window of the store, Merrick could see Betty Mitchell sweeping the day's dirt into a pile in the center of the room. He walked past once, stomping down the wooden sidewalk as though he was rushing to an emergency. When he got to the end of the row of shops, he hopped down onto the street and turned right, without thinking or knowing where he was going. He walked up the slight incline that occurred in this part of the town center. When it rained, this sloped street became a river; he could still see the furrows in the dirt from the last big storm they'd had. Soon it would be snow they'd be contending with and his job would become that much more challenging. The previous winter had been hard on everyone; several people had moved away, back to the coast where the climate was milder and where amenities were easier to come by. Living out here in a new province, with the paint hardly dry on the few buildings they had, was not easy.

But Merrick loved it. He loved the wide open space and the feelings of possibility and opportunity available to him. As a boy growing up on a farm in the Ottawa valley, he had known from a very early age what his future held. He and his brothers would take over the farm from his father, and they would work the earth until they died. Someone, probably his mother, would find him a wife, and they in turn would produce children that would do the same as their parents had done.

By the age of ten he couldn't bear this idea. It stifled him, made him feel a panicky sensation. He felt like there were birds trapped inside his chest anytime he thought of his future. By thirteen he had started talking to his brothers about it, wondering if they felt the same way. They looked at him like he had two heads. His oldest brother, Daniel, was courting a girl and planning to marry her. The look of peace and satisfaction on his brother's face whenever he talked of his future made Merrick question his own sanity. Why couldn't he feel that way? It would be so much easier if he did.

He waited for the feeling of panic to go away. Waited to feel like Dan did, and like Michael did as well, who'd married a year after Dan. Waited to feel secure and satisfied and pleased with the bounty that surrounded him. For it was true that the Merrick farm was one of the most successful in the valley. Callum Merrick often repeated the story of starting out with nothing and buying his first small plot of land with the wages he'd scraped together working several jobs. The elder Merrick had worked incredibly hard and had prospered. The man didn't know the meaning of a day off, or even an hour. And he'd married a woman with a work ethic just like his. They were good people. Not affectionate or nurturing - who had time for that? But Jack Merrick had known he was loved.

So why did he want to leave it all behind?

He had never been able to reconcile that question inside himself. It just was.

The day after he turned sixteen, he kissed his mother goodbye, knowing it was not likely he would ever see her again. She was the only one he told that he was leaving. He felt she deserved to know; he couldn't just up and disappear on her.

She was shattered, naturally, but she didn't seem surprised. She brushed a strand of his dark, curly hair out of his eyes and touched his cheek. "You'll do very well," she said, "you're just like your father."

Merrick was stunned. For his entire childhood he had wondered why he could not align himself with his father's dream. He assumed it was because they were so different.

June Merrick saw the confusion in her boy's eyes and chuckled. "How d'ye think we ended up here, son? Your father's a dreamer, too. He wanted better things for himself than working for his old man in Aberdeen. This farm and this family is his dream. Now you must go find your own."

So he had left with his mother's blessing, which fueled him for many cold and hard seasons. It was a long and difficult way from Ottawa to British Columbia, and it had taken him four years to get there. But the moment he stepped onto the dock in what was then called Granville, he knew he was home. Somewhere in this new, wild place was the thing he'd been searching for.

It was a twisty, uncertain road from farmer's son to police constable, and he fell into the job by accident. But it suited him perfectly and he was grateful for it every day. He loved the responsibility he felt for the town and its people; the courageous, the lost, the searchers, and the slightly mad. He loved that every day was different and totally unpredictable. The routine of the farm had nearly killed him with boredom, but here he was never bored.

Especially not since Miss Julia Thom had arrived. Now there was a burr under his saddle blanket. He was not practiced with women, that much was for certain. His wife, Charlotte, who he'd accidentally fallen in love with, had been strong-willed, but this trait had been paired with a pleasant and peaceful nature. When she died eighteen months earlier,

Merrick had been devastated. But he had borne the loss with a grim Scottish determination that his father would have been proud of. The constable didn't miss a day of work. And strangers coming into town would never know he'd suffered such a blow.

In the past six weeks since Julia Thom arrived in Horse, Merrick spent a fair amount of time being annoyed with her. She had helped him solve the puzzle of a break-in at the Mitchell's general store, for which he was equal parts grateful and irritated. The school teacher tended to stick her nose in where it didn't belong, at least when it came to Merrick's job as the sole officer of the law for hundreds of miles.

He was floundering. His reaction to her just now in the livery was overblown, and he knew it. But he was lost as to how to deal with her. The one person he thought could help him was his mother. But it would take too long to explain everything to her in a letter, post it and wait to receive her advice back in the mail. The answer might not reach him for six months.

It was his job to understand people. He'd had to develop that skill quickly when he'd left the farm. He would not have survived the long trip across the prairies and then over the Rocky Mountains if he had not learned how to read people; how to know their intentions almost before they did. His job as a police officer depended on this skill as well. He considered it one of his strengths. And yet, Julia...

He needed immediate help and there was only one person he felt even remotely comfortable broaching this subject with.

Merrick paced on the gentle hill for a few more moments and then made his decision. He charged back down toward Main Street and leapt up onto the sidewalk. In a few long strides he was at the Mitchell's door. He pulled it open and marched inside with such force that Betty Mitchell startled and nearly dropped her broom.

"Good heavens, Constable Merrick. You gave me a fright."

But she was smiling, as usual. The Mitchells both seemed to have two of the sunniest personalities in the west.

"Sorry. Sorry, Betty." Merrick pulled the door closed behind him with more care and turned to her, taking his hat off.

"What can I help you with?" Betty walked over and leaned the broom on one of the low glass counters that formed a U-shape around the store.

Suddenly Merrick was shy. He couldn't just blurt out his problem. Besides, what was it, really? Was he angry with Julia or worried about her? He needed another moment to gather his courage.

Stalling, he said the first thing that came to him. "I need some twine."

"Twine? Right." Betty walked through a gap in the countertops and reached for a basket on one of the shelves that lined the store walls on every side. She fished around in the basket and came up with a ball of twine slightly smaller than her fist. "Will that do?"

"That's fine." Merrick was still trying to collect himself, trying to find the right phrasing for his question. Betty was moving too efficiently. He needed more time. "And some, uh, some of those strawberry preserves you had the other day."

"Certainly." Betty made her way around the back of the counter, aiming for a different set of shelves. "You haven't gone through that other jar already have you?"

Damn this woman and her excellent memory. He had just bought a jar of preserves two days ago. "This one is a gift." Merrick winced inwardly, not sure this reasoning would hold up. He felt like a criminal who panics at the first line of questioning.

"A gift," Betty put the glass jar on the counter and set his twine down beside it. "That's lovely. Who's it for?"

"Walt Sheehan." The name was out of Merrick's mouth before he knew what he was doing.

Curiosity now appeared in Betty's eyes, and the corners of her mouth turned up just slightly. "One ball of twine and one jar of preserves for Mr. Sheehan. Anything else?"

They were standing face-to-face now, Betty on one side of the counter and Merrick on the other. The store was empty but for the two of them. And it was nearly five o'clock, closing time, so Merrick doubted anyone else would barge in on them. He had a clear path, and might not get another moment like this. If he could just figure out a way to capitalize on it. Betty watched him thinking, the look of amusement still making her eyes twinkle.

"Constable Merrick!"

Merrick jerked like someone had touched his back with a hot poker. Christopher Mitchell appeared from the storeroom behind the retail part of the store. He had a wooden crate of apples in his arms and his usual wide smile in place.

Merrick tried to rally. "Christopher. How are you today?"

"Very well. Very well, thank you." Mitchell set the crate down and began moving the apples from it into a display basket at the front of the store.

Merrick wasn't sure what to do. His moment was gone. There was no way he was going to talk to both the Mitchells about his failings to understand Julia and his desire to stop her from interfering in his work. Let alone his inexplicably elevated levels of frustration and anger at dealing with her. And his confusion about why she drove him so mad.

He looked back at Betty. "That's all thanks, Betty. Just the twine and the preserves." He fished around in his pockets for some coins.

"Righto." She took his money and handed him the items, one in each hand.

"Have a good evening, then, Constable." Christopher nodded at him as Merrick opened the door and stepped across the threshold.

WALT SHEEHAN's day was coming to a close. The light began to fade earlier every day and he had stalls to clean before he would take himself to Finnegan's for a pint and some of Caroline's stew. He put the finishing touches on an intricate fire poker he was making to sell. It embarrassed him slightly to work on something beautiful, but it also soothed a place in his soul that was in desperate need of some kindness. He had an idea to form the handle in narrow, twisting strips of iron so that it looked like a pine cone. He hadn't been able to get it quite right yet, but he was getting closer to the image he had in his mind.

He never worked on the set of fire tools during the day; it was a private project he spent just a few minutes on each week when he could spare the time from pounding out nails and shoveling horse manure. When he wasn't working on the set he kept them hidden deep in the shadows under his work bench, covered by an old horse blanket.

He was bent over the anvil, spinning and forming the piece of iron, his attention utterly consumed by the task. He heard footsteps enter the forge. His head lifted and he saw Merrick standing by the workbench at the front of the building. The constable held up a glass mason jar with a scrap of cotton fabric tied over its lid.

"Bought you a jar of preserves," Merrick said, setting the jar down on the table with considerable force. He held up his other hand. "And some twine." He set this down as well and then whirled around and stalked out the front door.

What the hell was that about? Walt thought. He shrugged to himself and bent again to his task.

CHAPTER EIGHT

Finnegan's hotel and restaurant was far and away the nicest place in Horse. The hotel had been built by Edgar Finnegan, who had come from money and was looking to make an impression on British Columbia. Edgar had had the good fortune to marry a woman as driven as he was and together they had built the business into the going concern it was. Edgar and Caroline were looking forward to the day the rumored railway spur line from Kelowna would be finished. Until then, they bided their time and perfected their particular brand of stern, but generous, service.

Julia arrived just as the supper hour was beginning. Millie and Billy Jones were seated at their usual table, and two men in stockmen's suits sat at a table for four near the front window.

"May I help you, Miss Thom?" Edgar called from behind the bar, where he was drying glasses.

It wasn't entirely proper for a lady to enter a restaurant and bar alone, but the rules of propriety tended to bend a little more in a town like Horse, when women who were on their own had no choice but to do some things by themselves. As long as she stayed on the main floor and didn't even glance in the direction of the wide, wooden staircase that led up to the hotel rooms on the second and third floor, Julia should be able to avoid scandal.

She approached the bar. "I'm looking for Lily, Edgar. Is she around?"

Lily Cecil was very new to Horse. Julia wasn't actually sure they'd been formally introduced. But Julia did know that Lily worked part-time as a server and dishwasher for the Finnegans.

"She is, lass. She's in the kitchen. D'ye want me to get her?"

"Is it okay if I go back there? I don't want to interrupt her work."

"Aye. Go on back," Edgar nodded toward the kitchen door. "Tell the missus I said it was okay if she asks. Not that I have any sway around here." He winked at Julia.

The kitchen was almost as large as the dining room. A big stone fireplace equipped with rotisserie spits filled one end of the room. At the other end were two huge cooking stoves. Down the center of the room was a long wooden table, upon which now lay the makings of several apple pies. Lily Cecil was dressed in a flowered cotton top with short sleeves and a long black skirt that touched the top of her buttoned boots. Over this she had a stained white apron tied around her waist. A flowered kerchief that looked like it was perhaps made from the same material as her blouse covered her shoulder-length, almost white blonde hair.

She was a tiny thing. When Julia had first seen her, two weeks previously at church, she wondered if she would see the girl at school on Monday morning. But then a young and ragged-looking man sat down beside Lily and by the way they put their heads together when they spoke made Julia realize that they were married. Millie Jones, who made gossip her livelihood, confirmed to Julia after the service that these were the Cecils. Alan worked for the Double A Ranch outside town and Lily had just secured the job with the Finnegans.

"Charity, I call that," Millie said with a sniff in her voice.

"Why do you say that?" Julia asked.

"The Finnegans will work all the hours God sends. They don't need any help - they've got the Chinaman cooking for them and the two of them doing everything else." She lowered her voice, "They took pity on the girl because her husband is a lazy so-and-so and has been fired from every job he's taken on so far. The pair are destitute."

Given that the Cecils had been in Horse's vicinity for all of ten minutes, Julia wasn't sure how Millie could know this.

Millie continued, reading Julia's mind, "Katherine at the O'Brien Ranch is Lily's aunt by marriage. She convinced her husband to hire Alan and then further twisted Edgar Finnegan's arm to hire the girl. Too much generosity, if you ask me. It's not good for the soul. We all have to make our own way in the world." This was rich, coming from a woman whose family owned half of the city of Victoria on Vancouver Island and who had been handed every possible advantage in life, including a husband who treated her far better than she deserved.

But this visit in the kitchen of the restaurant was the first time Julia had been close to Lily. She watched the girl roll out pastry for a moment, noticing a fine bruise on one of her wrists. "Mrs. Cecil?" she said.

The girl, for she could hardly be a day over eighteen years old, looked up, slightly startled.

"I'm Miss Thom, from the school."

"Yes, hello Miss Thom," Lily straightened her spine and wiped her hands on her apron, "I'm not sure where Mrs. Finnegan is. Shall I find her for you?"

"It's you I'm here to see, Lily. May I call you Lily?"

The girl nodded.

Mr. Hunter had no memory of who had beaten him. With

the stained glove as her only clue, Julia wanted to find out more. She knew almost nothing of Hunter, beyond his occupation and his name, but she remembered that at the dance on Saturday night, Lily Cecil had seemed familiar with Hunter.

Julia took a small breath and softened her energy somewhat. She knew she had a tendency to come across like a stallion with the bit in its teeth when she was on a mission. It served her schoolteacher persona well, and kept the children in line, but sometimes she knew people felt she was a bit fierce. Lily Cecil looked like someone who needed a soft touch on the reins rather than a strong hand. "Please call me Julia."

The girl nodded again, concern and a slight fearfulness shrouding her eyes.

"I wanted to ask you about the dance on Saturday night. I believe I saw you there."

"You did." Lily's tone made the statement almost a question.

"You were standing with James Hunter at one point, I believe."

Now the girl's brow creased with a lack of understanding. She shook her head slightly. "I don't know anyone by that name."

"James Hunter, the watchmaker?" No recognition lit Lily's eyes, so Julia continued to explain. "You both were standing near the punch table, sort of close to the front of the class...that is, the far end of the room, farthest from the door. After Mr. Hunter and I came in from outside?" She made it a question.

Still Lily's brows were creased. She wiped her hands again on her apron and glanced around, perhaps looking for Mrs. Finnegan to rescue her.

Julia continued, undeterred, "Mr. Hunter is about this tall." She held her right hand just above the top of her own head. "He dresses very neatly and wears a nice watch chain."

Julia was struggling to describe the man. All gentlemen wore dark suits and most had whiskers.

"Oh, James!" Lily finally said, while Julia was grasping for what more to say. Lily gave a small laugh. "Mr. Hunter. Yes. Now I know who you mean."

Julia relaxed. Now they were on common ground. "Not that it's any of my business, but did you know Mr. Hunter before you arrived in Horse?"

"Um," Julia could see Lily thinking, "Yes. Yes, I did know him. We were at the same school in Granville, though he was a few years ahead of me."

"What a coincidence that you would both arrived here, then."

"It is." Lily nodded and waited with the patience of one who doesn't make many of their own decisions in life.

"Did you know Mr. Hunter was beaten badly yesterday?"

"Mrs. Finnegan told me, yes."

"Pardon me for being impertinent, but if you knew Mr. Hunter from your school days, do you know any reason why anyone would want to hurt him? He doesn't remember anything."

Lily's eyes grew slightly wider as she thought about this. She shook her head, but it was not a decisive shake.

"Do you know if Mr. Hunter knows anyone else in town, besides yourself?"

Again Lily shook her head.

Julia couldn't be sure if the young woman was shy or just not very intelligent. Her answers weren't satisfying.

Caroline Finnegan came into the room through back door, a basket of carrots and beets in her arms.

"Julia. How nice to see you."

Lily bent to her task again, rolling the wide wooden pin over the dough on the table.

Caroline put her basket down on the wide table in the

middle of the room. "Did you hear that Olivia Smith is having a baby?"

Distracted, Julia shook her head.

Caroline continued, talking about the Smith's joy at having their first child and how Mrs. Thoreson was already working on a quilt for the baby. Julia hardly heard her friend.

"...and then we'll get together once Christmas is over."

Julia snapped back to attention, "Pardon me?"

Caroline looked up from the basin where she was washing the carrots. "You're distracted today, aren't you? I said we'll have a tea once the baby is born, which will probably be after Christmas."

"Oh, yes. That will be lovely."

Lily continued making her apple tarts. She studiously avoided Julia's eyes, carefully placing apple slices into the little dough pockets she had made.

Julia excused herself and left the kitchen via the back door into the yard behind the hotel, her curiosity unsatisfied.

CHAPTER NINE

Overnight, Julia thought about her conversation with Lily Cecil. It had left her with a bad taste in her mouth, but she couldn't figure out why. Julia, who was becoming better at spotting a liar after six weeks of dealing with school-aged children who were always covering something up, didn't sense that Lily was lying. But still, the conversation left her with an odd, unsettled feeling.

She dressed quickly on Wednesday morning, wanting to make sure she had time to visit Merrick's office before she had to be at the school. One of these days, she muttered to herself, I'm going to have to get some new dresses, as a button fell off the sleeve of her favorite blouse, one with slightly puffed sleeves. Sewing had been her worst skill growing up. Her mother used to despair at Julia's crooked stitches and off-center buttons.

"How is a woman like you supposed to catch a husband if you're not even dressed properly?"

The secret was that Julia had no intention of 'catching' a husband. In those days she still had her heart set on being a lawyer like her father and back then the thought of marriage made her shiver.

As a model, her parents' marriage was satisfactory; they tended to mostly leave each other alone to live the lives each of them wanted. Julia's father, Judge Thom, spent most of his life traveling to preside over cases around the province and smoking cigars with his cronies in New Westminster. Her mother adored playing at being lady of the manor, and hosted teas and lunches for anyone who would sit still long enough. She supervised Julia's education, torturing governesses when Julia's piano playing or drawing was sub-par. Which was always because Julia only wanted to read and to sneak into her father's study to hear him talk about his cases.

"Dammit!" A button came off her other cuff. Quickly she pulled the blouse off and found another in her wardrobe that was not too wrinkled.

When she was completely dressed except for her boots, she pulled her riding jodhpurs on, up under her skirt, and then sat to button up her boots. If things went as planned, she would need the riding pants on immediately after school and didn't want to take the time to come home to change.

MERRICK WAS AT HIS DESK, though it was barely eight o'clock. He was hunched over a stack of papers, reading while eating an apple. The door to the office was propped open with the head of a hammer whose handle had broken off. The fall day was crisp and the air smelled wonderful. Merrick couldn't resist airing out the office, which had a faint odor of vomit from town drunk Arthur 'Sully' Sullivan's last overnight stay.

"Oh, good, you're here." Julia sped into the office, startling Merrick slightly, and sat down in one of the guest chairs that faced his desk.

Merrick's office was dark and a bit gloomy, which was too bad, for he was a fellow who loved bright sunlight. Although, in the heat of a North Okanagan summer, when temperatures could read 100 degrees in the shade, he was always glad for the north-facing windows. The floors were stained a dark color, as were the walls. Julia wondered, when she had first seen the room, if this had been intentional; this was not a place of frivolity. The men who were housed here temporarily, in the small, barred enclosure at the back of the room, were often not long for this world.

Several cabinets stood to attention behind Merrick, their drawers hanging open in some cases. The paperwork that flowed through a constable's office was endless; he was tax collector and notary public, birth and death registrar and local weather man. Dealing with criminal activity was most often the least of Merrick's worries.

Perpendicular to the desk, the telegraph table was set against one wall. Other than the mail, this was Horse's only means of communication with the outside world.

Julia noticed a fine layer of dust over everything that had not been moved recently, and a clean circle on the desk demarking where the apple Merrick was eating had been until moments ago. The constable's black, wide-brimmed hat was hanging on the coat tree in a corner. Merrick kept his suit jacket on in deference to the slight chill in the air from the open door. The small parlor stove at the back of the room was not lit.

Julia was amused to notice that Merrick's face fell when he looked up and saw her taking an uninvited seat. She'd realized the day before that she got quite a lot of enjoyment out of torturing the police constable. He did not appear to be someone who could be ruffled easily, and yet, she noticed he often seemed a little ruffled around her. She liked having this effect on someone so large and imposing.

She smiled at the man, "Good morning, Constable Merrick."

"Good morning, Miss Thom. Please tell me you've come in to ask about the stage coach schedule."

"I haven't, but tell me anyway."

Merrick watched her for a few beats. Finally he said, "I won't waste your time. Or mine. Why don't you tell me why you're here?"

"You mentioned that you were going out to the Double A Ranch today to question the drovers there about the interrupted..." she faltered slightly, and then rallied, "incident at the dance on Saturday night."

Merrick nodded, chewing slowly.

"I would like to propose something. But before I do, will you promise to listen to me without prejudice until I am finished?"

The constable thought about this for a moment. He swallowed. "I won't promise, but I'll try."

"Fair enough. Here's my suggestion: wait until school is finished today so that you can take me with you to the Double A."

"No way."

Julia was shocked by the rapid response. She began to speak but snapped her jaw shut and pursed her lips. When she opened them again her voice sounded grave. "Now, Constable, you promised to listen without prejudice and..."

Merrick interrupted her, "And I did. I thought about your idea and then I rejected it. I told you when you suggested going with me to the Green ranch that the idea was inappropriate. It's...it's... I don't even have a word for it. Miss Thom, I am an officer of the law. You are a civilian without the requisite legal authority to be questioning suspects with me. I cannot and will not take you with me to the Double A. There is nothing further to discuss."

"It's a fine afternoon for a ride, isn't it? The horses seem to be really enjoying themselves." Julia shifted her reins to one hand and patted Stanley's neck.

Merrick grunted at her, not wanting to agree, even though she was right.

She had worn him down and won the argument about taking her with him to the ranch. She'd pointed out that she was the only person who could potentially identify her would-be attackers and that without her the trip would be futile. Whoever Merrick spoke to would deny having been at the dance, and also deny threatening Julia. If he took her with him, he would save time and have a definitive answer to the question. His trip the day before to Middle Lake Ranch had been unsuccessful and every hour that he spent riding around to local ranches was another hour away from town. Finally, feeling caught between a rock and Julia Thom's torrent of words, he'd given in.

But he was not happy about it.

Julia liked it when Merrick sulked. She was learning to deal with the moods and upsets of the children in her classroom and dealing with Merrick at times just gave her more practice.

Walt joined them, and Julia was grateful for this. He so often provided a buffer between herself and Constable Merrick.

The three horses walked shoulder to shoulder, Julia's paint horse, Stanley, in between the two enormous animals on either side of her. Had the Double A been any further out of town, Julia's plan to have Merrick wait until after school to ride out would not have worked. But the ranch was within easy riding distance and the trio would make it back to Horse by supper time and before dark.

Julia inhaled deeply, appreciating the scents of dry grass and soil. Crickets chirped as they walked. A startled thrush flew up in front of the group, and all the horses flicked their ears forward to watch but stayed calm.

Julia was riding astride her horse, as she always did. Her long skirt flowed over Stanley's rump and the jodhpurs underneath it made her feel capable. She always felt less hampered by her gender when she was riding.

The silence and space allowed her to think and, unbidden, visual memories of the night of the dance came to mind. She could still smell the men who had grabbed her, their tobacco and dried sweat, the oddly sweet smell of the breath of First Man. Julia tried to push the images away but they popped up again, like corks in a bathtub. The shiny knife First Man had held to her face, its blade flashing in the night, despite the lack of light around them.

She readjusted her reins and tugged on her hat brim, trying to get away from her own thoughts. The men rode on silently and Julia tried to come up with a topic of conversation to distract herself. The group crested a hill and turned slightly to their left. The Double A house and barn came into sight. Julia estimated that they must be on the ranch's land already, for the house was set almost exactly in the middle of the property.

The sight of the buildings and a couple of figures walking around gave Julia some peace. Though she was reminded why they were there.

The three horses, eyeing the buildings and the potential for a snack, made their way toward the little cluster of buildings without much guidance.

The barn was much larger than the house; this was where Gerard Anker's energy went. It was a long, low building with a peaked roof and doors on both ends. Horses were kept here, and equipment. The cattle that were the ranch's mainstay lived on the land, fattening up on the sweet grasses that abounded in the rich soil.

Merrick, Julia and Walt dismounted.

"Anker?" Merrick called.

The barn was quiet. They looked away toward the house, which was as grand as any that Julia had ever seen at home in New Westminster. It was like a beautiful doll house blown up to full size. Painted bright yellow with clean white trim around the windows and doors, it had a wide porch that ran all the way around the building. It was three stories high, with a decorative weather vane in the shape of a great blue heron at the mid-point of the roofline, giving the building the impression of even more height than it already had. The windows all glinted in the sunlight, and the tops of the porch columns were decorated with detailed woodwork that must have taken ages to create. The side of the house had a large kitchen garden with a white picket fence surrounding it and an arbor at each end. The decorative features of the building, which had no practical use and must have taken many man hours to build and install, all created an unmistakable impression of wealth.

"Good heavens," Julia said under her breath as she absorbed all there was to see.

"Mrs. Anker comes from a very wealthy family," Merrick said.

"You don't say," Julia muttered. She took a closer look at the weather vane. "Do I recognize your handiwork there, Walt?"

The blacksmith looked at her out of the corner of his eye and nodded just slightly.

A figure came out the front door onto the porch and waved at them. Though he didn't have children in her school Julia recognized the figure as Gerard Anker, proprietor of the Double A Ranch.

As he got closer to them, Julia could see that Anker was a tall man, though not as tall as Walt and Merrick. He moved somewhat stiffly, as though his feet or ankles were bothering him. His hairline was retreating, leaving a large and speckled forehead in its wake. Julia had only met the man once or twice before and was struck each time by his sparkly eyes. He perpetually looked as though he was up to some gentle kind of mischief.

"Gentlemen!" he called to the group, and then wiped at his mustache with the napkin he held in one hand. "What can I do for you? Oh, and Miss Thom. Excuse me, Miss, I didn't see you there. Like a rose between two thorns." Anker walked straight up to Julia and took one of her gloved hands in his and kissed her knuckles, an old-fashioned habit and one that seemed a bit odd, but Julia was touched.

Anker stepped back and looked at the two men, "What can I do for you fellows today?"

Merrick spoke first. "Mr. Anker, I don't know if you heard that there was a bit of an incident at the dance on Saturday night?"

"The missus was saying something about that yesterday, but I didn't catch it all. Something involving you, Miss Thom." He nodded toward her and then looked back to Merrick.

"Miss Thom was threatened by two men that night. Outside, near the outhouse."

"I'm sorry to hear that, Miss." Anker did look genuinely grieved.

Merrick continued. "We get the impression from Miss Thom's description that the men who threatened her may have been drovers. I'm asking around, looking to speak to the men you might have working for you, to see if Miss Thom can identify them."

Julia could see Anker processing this information. He rocked back on his heels and then forward again. "I see, I see," he said. "You think it might have been some of my men?"

"No, I don't, Mr. Anker. I don't have any idea who it was." Merrick was moving delicately. "But what we'd like to do is eliminate the possibility. And the only way to do that is for Miss Thom to have a look at your drovers."

Anker thought about this for a moment. He looked at Julia again, and then back to Merrick. Walt had stood silently this whole time. If Anker was curious about why he was there, he didn't ask.

Making a decision, Anker eventually said, "Okay then. Come with me. The men happen to be close at hand today." He turned and began walking west, away from the house and barn. Merrick, Julia and Walt followed, leading their horses. Merrick took the lead, walking beside Anker, while Julia and Walt fell in behind them.

"Nervous?" Walt said after a moment.

Julia glanced at him, appreciating his perceptiveness. "A little."

"It's good you're doing this. Despite Merrick's objections, I think it's better this way. More definitive."

The group was walking along a fence line and soon came upon four men who were repairing a post. Julia's breath caught in her throat when she saw them. They were like cutouts of one another. Each one wiry and spare, with a wide brimmed hat on. As Julia got closer she could see some distinguishing characteristics; one had a russet colored mustache and beard, another had eyes that looked in slightly different directions.

The men stopped their work and looked at the group approaching them.

"Mr. Anker," said a man with a black beard and small dark eyes, addressing his employer.

"Gents!" Anker began, "How are you getting along with this fence post? Almost done?" Anker made small talk with the men for a few minutes, easing them into the matter at hand.

While he did so, Julia watched the men, looking for clues that would match one or two of them to her attack. One of the men was quite short, not much taller than Julia herself. She eliminated him right away because the men who'd threatened her had definitely been taller than this. The other three, though, were possibilities. They were each the right height and build. While they spoke to Anker, Julia listened carefully to their voices.

Anker looked at Merrick at one point and Merrick took over. "Gentlemen, I wonder if you could help me with my enquiry. We're wanting to eliminate you as suspects in the attack on Miss Thom, here," he gestured to Julia, "last Saturday night."

The men each turned and looked at Julia. She held their gaze but her grip on Stanley's reins tightened.

Merrick continued. "Could you each please say your name?" He knew that the best descriptor Julia had was the sound of her attackers' voices. "Starting with you, sir." Merrick nodded his head at the drover with the russet beard.

In turn, each man said his name. Julia held in her mind the event from Saturday night and tried to match it to what she was experiencing now. When the men had finished she met Merrick's eyes and shook her head almost imperceptibly.

"That's fine. Thank you, gentlemen." Merrick turned to Anker, "We can leave you in peace now, Mr. Anker. Thank you for your help."

"My pleasure, son. Anything to see the blaggards who attacked Miss Thom brought to rights." He winked at Julia.

As THE THREE figures rode back to Horse, Julia was quiet, absorbed in her own thoughts. She had been more anxious about the task of meeting Anker's drovers than she'd realized. Now that the meeting was over, it brought her some peace to know the men at the Double A were not her assailants. She felt her shoulders begin to loosen. At the same time, there were still lots of men on the surrounding ranches who could be the culprits. Julia was loathe to admit to herself how much she'd been affected by the events of Saturday night; she'd been studiously avoiding her feelings ever since.

Now, with Merrick and Walt on either side of her, and the

quiet of the early evening surrounding them, she recognized that the mystery of Mr. Hunter's beating was doing an excellent job of distracting her from her own discomfort. Though she was horrified about what had happened to the clockmaker, she was pleased to have a puzzle to focus her attention on. She took a deep breath and shifted slightly in her saddle.

Out of the corner of her eye she saw Merrick watching her.

"What?" she said, turning toward him.

"I'm worried," he said.

"Why?"

"You were looking solemn but now you've got that determined expression on your face. The one that makes me so nervous."

"Oh good," Julia said, smiling for the first time since they'd left Horse. "Someone needs to keep you on your toes, Constable. It might as well be me."

CHAPTER TEN

Every day before he headed home to his cold little house near the lake, Merrick stopped by Walt's livery to help muck out stalls. He began with Earl's, of course, but then depending on how many guest horses were occupying the other stalls, he helped with those as well.

On Thursday afternoon Merrick found Walt repairing and replacing the girth strap and some other leather on an old saddle. He had a sawhorse in front of the livery, with the saddle straddling it and his chair pulled up to it. Beside him, in a basket, were spare leather parts of varying degrees of worn-ness. The three dogs that were Walt's constant companions at the livery were circling around, sniffing and lifting their legs on fence posts. When Merrick approached, they came to him to say hello, pressing themselves against his legs and thumping his calves with their tails. They were each medium-sized, with ears that flopped over and long tails. They were mottled with black, white, brown and tan, and had dark, liquid eyes that lit up whenever anyone paid them any attention. Merrick had often wondered if they were litter-mates. All three dogs were developing winter coats. As Merrick leaned over to pet each of them, he could feel the thickening in their fur.

Greeting ritual complete, Merrick went into the livery and grabbed the chair that was one of three that were always present, close to the doorway. It used to be two chairs that occupied the space, but Merrick noticed recently that another had been added. He couldn't decide if he liked this development or not.

He set the chair down with a slight thump a few feet away from Walt's chair. One of the dogs came and put its head in Merrick's lap so that he would stroke its ears. The big man obliged, and the dog closed its eyes with pleasure.

The two men were quiet. Nothing was required of Merrick in this moment and he was enjoying that feeling. Merrick spent much of his life listening and responding to the problems of the people around him. Walt never required him to be a police constable.

Finally, Merrick said, "Might rain tomorrow."

"Aye," Walt replied, hunched over, squinting at the piece of leather he was sewing.

"We could use the rain."

"Aye."

They were quiet for a few moments more. The dog in Merrick's lap was sated; he pulled away and went to wrestle with one of his cronies. The two dogs gargled and gently growled at one another while they mouthed each other's necks and bumped one another with their chests, lifting their front paws to try to headlock one another.

"What was your impression at the Double A yesterday?"

Walt lifted his eyes and looked at Merrick, his fingers tugging at a thick line of thread he was using to sew two pieces of leather together. He looked back at his work, thinking. Merrick waited.

Finally he spoke, answering Merrick's question with a question, "About Anker's men?"

Merrick nodded.

"I wouldn't trust any of them as far as I could throw them.

But I didn't notice any guilt among them, if that's what you're asking."

"It is. I didn't see any guilt in them either. But impressions can be wrong."

"Julia didn't recognize any of them."

"No." Merrick shook his head and looked down at his boots, thinking. "She paid close attention to their voices but didn't notice any familiarity when they spoke."

Walt continued sewing, pushing the needle through the leather with his thick fingers. He made sure to keep his eyes on his work when he next spoke. "I noticed Julia convinced you to take her with us when we went to the ranch. I didn't think that was the plan."

Merrick grunted quietly. "It wasn't." He was quiet now for a few moments, and it was Walt's turn to wait his friend out. When Merrick spoke again his voice was low, almost as though he was speaking to himself. "I find Miss Thom challenging to deal with."

"How so?"

"Well...she pushes her way into things, like the trip to the ranch yesterday. I haven't known her very long, granted, but I don't think I like her very much."

Walt looked up from his work. "Really?" He sounded skeptical. "I thought you two were getting along a bit better."

"I wish we were," Merrick shook his head slightly, "But she's a bit of a burr under my saddle blanket at the moment. I can't seem to get her to understand that police business is my affair, and that she should leave that work to me and stick to school teaching."

Finished with his repair work, Walt stood up. All three dogs froze and looked at him, their ears perked, eyes alert. He picked up the sawhorse and spun it around so the opposite side was facing him. When he sat down again to work on the leather on this new side, the dogs relaxed and resumed wrestling. "She's stepping on your toes."

"Aye, she is. And repeatedly." Merrick stood up and began pacing in front of the livery. "What if every citizen got involved like she did? What if I had people running around, looking into cattle theft? We'd all be tripping over one another, and I'd get nothing done. It can't be that way. I can't have other people trying to do my job."

Walt nodded, listening attentively, letting his friend vent.

"What if you had people coming in to the smithy, picking up your tools, trying to form their own horse shoes and nails?" Merrick looked at Walt, enjoying his own metaphor. "You couldn't work that way."

"Right."

"And I can't work this way either." Merrick stopped his pacing and leaned on the back of the wooden chair he'd been occupying. "I need to tell her. I need to sit her down and let her know she can't interfere any longer. It's over. I'm done indulging her amateur detective work."

"Excellent. A night in the stocks might do her some good."

Merrick glanced at his friend, "We don't use stocks."

"Mebbe we should."

Walt stood up and lifted the saddle off the sawhorse by its horn. "C'mon then you lazy bastard. That horse shit isn't going to shovel itself."

CHAPTER ELEVEN

Most of Julia's pupils lived within Horse's town limits, and they walked to and from school. Three out of the class of eleven lived outside of town on ranches. Harry Hewitt and Peter Little lived on adjoining properties about four miles outside of town.

At three o'clock on Thursday, when Julia was just wrapping up for the day, she heard footsteps coming up the wooden staircase at the front of the school. The door opened and Harry Hewitt's father stepped into the alcove where the children hung their coats.

All the children's heads swiveled to look at him and adorably the man blushed. "Don't mind me, Mrs. Thom," he said. "I was in town and just thought I'd pick up the boys and take them home on the wagon with me, rather than making them walk." He always called Julia "Mrs." and she never corrected him. She suspected it made him feel more comfortable chatting with her if they both pretended she was married.

Harry waved at his father.

"That's fine, Mr. Hewitt. We're about finished for the day." Julia made sure the older children understood their reading assignment for the night and then dismissed the group.

Mr. Hewitt stepped into the classroom to get out of the way of the multi-limbed monster that had now crowded around the coat hooks. He grinned at Julia. "I don't know how you do it all day with these ruffians. One is by far too much for me and Mrs. Hewitt to manage."

"Oh, they're no trouble at all, Mr. Hewitt." Julia said, which was not entirely true.

Mr. Hewitt was a slight man and didn't look like someone suited to farming life at all. He looked like he'd be much more comfortable working in a bank or a fine hotel. He was wiry, like a sapling, and not very tall. His complexion always looked red and raw, even when he wasn't blushing. He had dark circles under his eyes, but Julia wasn't sure if that was from exhaustion or just the natural state of the thin skin there. He was a jolly man though, quick to laugh and always kind with his words.

The children evaporated, leaving just the two boys waiting for Mr. Hewitt. The man was in no rush to leave, though. He usually took the opportunity to chat to Julia, starved, perhaps, for town gossip and interaction with an adult other than his wife.

Julia always obliged with whatever tidbits she had that wouldn't cause offense should they get back to the person who they were about. Today she shared that the fundraising for the church was going well and Pastor Thoreson thought they would probably be able to break ground in the spring.

"The town is growing at quite a pace, isn't it? If we can have a church and this schoolhouse."

"Very true, Mr. Hewitt."

News gratefully received, Mr. Hewitt made motions to leave. "Come on, boys. Let's get a move on and let Mrs. Thom get on with her day."

As Mr. Hewitt herded the boys down the steps, Julia walked with him. He was halfway down the staircase when he turned and said, "I was very sorry to hear about Mr. Hunter. That was just terrible."

"Wasn't it? Shocking."

Hewitt shook his head, rolling his soft cap in his hands. "He's a good man, Hunter. Quiet. Keeps to himself. But he's always polite and friendly. I like the man."

"I do too, Mr. Hewitt."

"I understand you found him?"

Julia nodded. "I did. He was not in a good way."

"He's on the mend now though?"

"Yes. He's doing well. Betty Mitchell and I popped in this morning to see how he was doing. He's nervous about getting fat on all the bread and scones Betty is feeding him."

Hewitt grinned. "He could use a bit more meat on his bones, that man. He's a wee little thing, isn't he?" Julia thought this was amusing coming from the reed-thin Mr. Hewitt. But she made agreeing noises.

On the street, Julia saw Harry and Peter climb onto the front seat of Mr. Hewitt's wagon. The man in front of her put his hat on and walked down two more steps. He called over his shoulder, "He'll be missed at the poker game, that's for sure. He always had enough cash, and he's a <u>terrible</u> player." Hewitt chuckled. "I won't be there, but they'll miss him tonight."

"Poker game?" Julia asked, "I thought gambling was illegal."

"Aye it is. But don't tell Jack Merrick that. He's a regular too." Mr. Hewitt went through the gate into the street and climbed up into the wagon. The boys waved as they drove off and Julia waved back, though her thoughts were elsewhere.

She had no idea such a game existed in town, and she suspected that was intentional. Gambling was not something ladies participated in or even acknowledged. And Mr. Hunter had participated. Julia's thoughts whirled. She knew so little about the man, and was determined to find out more in case that led her to the perpetrator of his beating. Even if the man himself wanted to let well enough alone, Julia couldn't bring herself to ignore the elephant in the room. Someone was bothered enough by something Hunter had done or said that he or they had beaten the man nearly to death. That was not an event Julia was willing to stand by and let be forgotten. Even if Hunter hadn't saved her from the blaggards at the dance, she would be invested in solving the puzzle of his attacker.

And now, she thought, as she stepped back into the schoolhouse, *I'll bet those men at the poker table know something about Hunter. If he's at the game regularly, they might know more about him than anyone in town. I'm just going to have to winkle information out of them, whether they like it or not.*

CHAPTER TWELVE

Hewitt didn't say where the poker game was held. Just that it was on Thursday nights. As luck would have it, this was a Thursday.

When she thought about who might attend the game, Julia began running through a roster of the town's men. She was nearly certain that Christopher Mitchell didn't play in the game. Not because he was more refined than any of the other men that she might find there, but just that he was, in addition to being a businessman, a scholar. He loved to read and at every social event he would corner Julia at least once so they could discuss the latest Greek play he was reading or the newest work by Mark Twain. Julia loved these conversations, as Christopher was the only person in Horse she could talk to about themes in literature and character development. She knew that Christopher spent any waking moment when he wasn't working in or on his store, in his upholstered chair in his and Betty's home above the shop, reading. He read each night, Betty said, until he fell asleep in the chair, at which point his wife nudged him off to bed.

Julia stood on the school steps considering who else she could talk to about the game. She fully intended to discover its location and then crash the game this very evening. Her mind sorted through the potential players. Mayor Jones was certainly involved. The man was always desperate for an excuse to spend time away from his wife, though he would never admit such a thing aloud. Julia shuddered at the thought of trying to find out from his wife, Millie, if he was involved. She didn't want to get the mayor into any more trouble than he already got into nearly every day.

Pastor Thoreson was definitely not involved.

Walt and Merrick almost certainly were but she refused to go directly to Merrick for information, since he seemed to be annoyed by her very presence these days.

She thought a bit more and then landed on the obvious solution. The one place in town where everyone's business was known.

JULIA FOUND Mr. and Mrs. Eng where they invariably always were: working over huge steaming pots of wet clothes. The cauldrons they used for laundry were so large Julia was almost sure she could bathe in one. The Engs absolutely could; perhaps both of them in one pot.

The couple nodded to her as one as she walked in. They wore almost identical stern expressions but Julia had always found the Engs to be friendly. Though it was often challenging to communicate with them through the barrier of language; Julia didn't speak Mandarin and the Engs didn't speak much English. Julia often wondered if they understood more than they let on.

This, in fact, was the reason she was there in the humid shop in the first place. Though the Engs didn't participate in many, if any, town social events, everyone in town knew them and many used their laundry services. Walt brought the linens from the livery here every week. And the single men in town, like Merrick, Walt and Sully, had the Engs do all their laundry, since they didn't have a wife at home to do it. And, in fact, Julia herself brought her laundry to the Engs each week. Working all day left her no time for the days-long process of washing all her bedding and clothes. Her mother would be horrified to know Julia spent some of her hard-earned wages this way, but Julia was damned if she was going to spend what precious time off she had up to her elbows in hot water and Borax. It was enough to keep her house reasonably clean and food on the table, without adding laundry into the mix.

"Mr. Eng," she said, making a little bob with her head, "Mrs. Eng. How are you today?"

The couple smiled at her and continued stirring.

"You took lon-lee," Mrs. Eng said. "No more." She made a sweeping away motion with her hand.

"Yes, thank you," Julia made an exaggerated nod, in the pantomime style of people conversing across a language barrier. "I'm looking for some information." She waited, letting the four syllable word sink in.

The Engs continued to stir.

Julia mulled over how best to ask for what she wanted in as few words as possible. "Poker," she finally said. "Cards." She mimed dealing out a hand of cards.

Mr. Eng looked at his wife and then back to Julia. His wispy eyebrows came together above the bridge of his nose. He shook his head.

Julia pretended to shuffle a deck of cards between her gloved hands, and then made the dealing motion again. "There's a card game somewhere in town tonight. Where is it?" She realized she was raising her voice, as though talking louder would help the Engs to understand her.

Both halves of the couple were mute. They exchanged a glance and shrugged and then looked back at Julia. Waiting for her to make some sense, it seemed. Julia thought that was unlikely to happen.

For lack of anything else to do, she began to babble, which

was often her default course of action when she was frustrated. Her story about James Hunter flooded out; how he had saved her when she was nearly attacked at the dance on Saturday night, how he had been so gracious with her when she needed her grandmother clock fixed. Later, Julia would realize that at this point in the story she made a motion like a swinging pendulum with her arms and then sang a bit of the melody of the Westminster chimes. The Engs faces began to reflect their concern that they might have a demented woman in their shop.

But Julia carried on, undeterred. She could hear herself talking too much and couldn't stop. "Then, just as I was about to leave his shop, I heard Mr. Hunter groan from behind the counter. I found him, beaten to a pulp and had to get Constable Merrick to help me take him to Dr. Parker's office. He's going to be fine, but I'm trying to figure out who would have done such a thing. I know so little about Mr. Hunter. He's so new to town. Almost as new as I am. But no one deserves such treatment. I heard about the poker game and I'm wondering..."

She ground to a halt. The oppressive heat and steam of the laundry tubs was affecting her. She was sure her face must be running with sweat and she wanted to undo the top button of her blouse.

The Engs continued to stir and watch her, like she was an exotic animal they hadn't encountered before.

Julia recognized that she was defeated. "Well, thank you," she said. "I'll be back next Monday, as usual, with my laundry."

She turned to go and as she did a rapid fire torrent of Mandarin erupted from Mrs. Eng. Julia waited while the couple exchanged many paragraphs, if not chapters, of discourse. They gestured occasionally toward Julia. Mrs. Eng's voice got louder and more insistent. Mr. Eng volleyed back, but he was no match for his wife. There was a crescendo with both of them talking urgently at once and then suddenly, like someone had turned off a switch, silence. Only the bubbling of the laundry pots.

The couple looked back at Julia. A few seconds ticked by. Then a few more. Julia waited, unsure as to what was happening. Perhaps the conversation had nothing to do with her. She imagined they'd tuned her out as soon as she'd started babbling in long, rushed sentences.

Mrs. Eng then startled Julia with a short, sharp comment directed at the side of her husband's head. Then she poked him in the shoulder with one strong finger.

Mr. Eng turned to his wife and made a shushing motion and then turned back toward Julia. He said one word that had several syllables, but Julia didn't catch it.

"I beg your pardon?"

Mr. Eng said the word again, but it was indecipherable to Julia.

"I'm sorry, Mr. Eng, I don't underst...."

"Finnegan's!" Mrs. Eng nearly shouted and made Julia jump. The word was as clear as any spoken yet, either by Julia or the Engs.

Julia's face broke into a wide smile. "Thank you," she said, backing out of the shop, nodding and smiling, "thank you!"

CHAPTER THIRTEEN

Caroline Finnegan was behind the bar, which was not entirely unusual, but not commonplace either. Lily Cecil was walking two dinner plates out to a couple Julia didn't recognize, whose heads were bent together, chatting quietly. Julia nodded to Lily on her way by and walked up to the bar with more confidence than she felt.

"I'm joining the poker game tonight, Caroline. Where is it?"

Caroline looked at Julia with her clear green eyes and snorted, "The hell you are, Julia Thom. You're the schoolteacher and a woman of good breeding. I will not send you into a room with those four dunderheads." Then she paused, catching herself. "What poker game?"

"It seems I'm the last person in town to know about it. And now I want in."

Caroline stood her ground, leaning on the bar with both hands and pushing her face toward Julia. "No."

Julia leaned in herself, the bar's edge pressing into her ribs. She spoke quietly, but with clarity, "If you don't tell me where it is, I'll make sure to mention to Millie Jones next time I see her that you were admiring her feathered hat the other day and were wanting her to teach you how to make such things."

The two women locked eyes. Julia knew she had Caroline over a barrel. Caroline had no time or patience for either couture or Millie Jones. Julia knew that Millie got under Caroline's skin more than most. And further, that Millie could sense it and would take any opportunity to get closer to Caroline and win her over.

Julia refused to blink. She watched ideas and questions swirl in her friend's eyes.

Finally Caroline said, "You will not. You're too nice to do that to me."

"The jury's still out on whether I'm nice, but I'll tell you for sure what I am tonight: I'm desperate and determined. I'm trying to find out who beat James Hunter."

There was another slight pause while Caroline considered this. Then she stood up straight, pulling herself away from the bar. The game was lost. Julia swore to herself; here she'd come to win at poker and hadn't even been able to bluff the gate-keeper. She prepared to turn and walk away.

"Room eight," Caroline said, looking stern.

Julia took a deep breath. "Thank you."

"They won't like you being there."

Julia expected this was true. The men's poker game was probably like a secret club and appealing as such.

Caroline continued, "But you tell them this. If they don't let you join I won't be bringing up sandwiches and beer throughout the night. They can feed themselves and the bar and kitchen will be closed to them." She nodded her head once, sharply.

"Thank you, Caroline." Julia smiled and turned to leave.

Caroline stopped her before she reached the bottom of the staircase. "You wouldn't have told Millie that lie about me liking her hat, would you?" the proprietress asked.

Julia shrugged and smiled. "We'll never know, will we?"

~

THE ROOM SMELLED of cigars and men.

When Julia opened the door to the room, Edgar Finnegan said, without looking up from his cards, "Sandwiches already? Christ, woman, we've hardly sat down."

Julia closed the door behind her. She wished she had a way to capture the comical look on each of the men's faces as they looked up at her.

The room was one of the hotel's standard guest rooms, but it had been altered for the men's purposes. There was no bed in it at all. The center of the room held a large round table, a match to the ones in the dining room below them. There was a wardrobe in one corner, and a tall dresser with a lamp burning on it. The bedside tables were there as well, though between them was not a bed but a narrow rectangular table with two partially empty bottles of whisky and a plate with just crumbs.

"I see you've got an empty place," Julia said, and sat down in what she assumed was James Hunter's spot.

Mayor Billy Jones had his cigar firmly planted between his lips. His round face sitting atop his round body always reminded Julia of a snowman. Now he looked even more like one, except instead of a carrot nose he had a cigar sticking out of his face.

Walt and Merrick were there. Walt grinned across the table at Julia and she could almost hear his glee. Merrick looked less thrilled to see her. He glared at her out from under his thick, black eyebrows.

"What're you doing, Miss Thom?" Finnegan asked. "You can't be here, lass."

Julia pulled off her gloves and laid them in her lap with her purse. "Deal me in, Edgar. I came to play, not talk."

Across the table Walt quietly snorted.

Mayor Billy looked at Finnegan and shifted his cigar to

one side of his mouth, "This is preposterous. She's a woman, for crying out loud."

Finnegan nodded and placed the deck he'd been shuffling down on the table in front of him. He folded his hands over it and pinned Julia down with a stare. "Miss Thom, I don't mean to be rude but this is a private game. Invitation only, you see."

"I do see." Julia nodded, folding her own hands together in front of her on the table. "And here's what else I see. An illegal gambling operation that I'm fairly confident Mrs. Jones doesn't know about. Or am I wrong about that, Mayor?"

The mayor shook his head sadly. "No. You're right. She thinks I'm here every Wednesday night talking town business with Edgar."

"I thought so," Julia nodded and smiled genially. She looked back to Edgar Finnegan. "Deal me in Edgar."

The host looked around the table at Walt, Merrick and Mayor Billy. She wasn't sure what he saw in his friends' eyes but he continued to hesitate.

Julia reached down into her lap and opened the clasp on her purse. She pulled out a wad of dollar bills and a few coins. The stack of bills was almost half an inch high.

Mayor Billy looked from the money up into Julia's face. "You heard the woman, Edgar," he said. "Deal her in."

JULIA WAS way out of her depth at the card table. She figured that out almost immediately.

She'd played a bit of poker with her father as a child, but only when her mother was out of the house. It was a secret between them and Julia loved these instances of something precious and secret that she had with her father. Poker was one of the devil's devices, so Mrs. Thom could never know about the games. From her father Julia learned strategy and bluffing. But they were rudimentary lessons; she had never played with more than one other player. This game in the smoky, stuffy hotel room was taking things to a whole new level.

As luck would have it, bluffing was a skill Julia had very recently been practicing. As a school teacher she had to be in command of the room of children she was in charge of, whether she felt in control or not. The children, she found out pretty quickly, could smell fear. They were like a pack of wolves on the hunt for the weakest member of the herd. It wasn't conscious with them, it seemed to be almost instinctual. Within three days of landing in Horse's schoolhouse, she had figured out that she could never, ever let her weak flank show. For her own safety, and ultimately for theirs, Julia needed to be in command at every moment. She wasn't cruel or mean, but she never let her guard down in front of the group.

This was the skill she applied now. The men were watching her, sussing her out, trying to find her weak spots and trying to intimidate her with their frosty glares. (All except Walt. He was enjoying himself immensely.) So Julia feigned confidence.

To her delight, she won the first round. This set the men back on their heels. Her presence was clearly removing some of the joy and banter they normally shared. They couldn't be themselves with Julia present and she knew that. She almost felt sorry for them.

While Merrick dealt the next hand, and while her luck held, Julia broached the reason she was there at all.

"Gentlemen, I understand James Hunter is a regular at this table."

The men grumbled agreement.

"Is he a good player?"

More grumbling but no actual words reached Julia's ears. She gathered the cards Merrick was flicking toward her under her palms and made an effort to ignore his hostility. Was his ill temper about her pushing in on the game, or because she had forced him to take her to the Double A ranch the other day? She shrugged and pressed on.

"Let me put it to you this way, then. Did he owe anyone money? Had he lost recently at the table?"

Merrick finished dealing and set the remains of the deck in the center of the table. "Why do you ask?" he said, gathering his own cards together and ordering them in his hands.

"Because someone beat him up and I'd like to know why."

Merrick laid his cards down and looked to his left. Mayor Billy indicated he wanted two cards. While he went around the table, questioning each player, Merrick's mouth formed a thin line. "I told you I talked to Hunter, didn't I? He doesn't want the matter investigated."

"You did tell me that, and I understand but..." she hesitated.

"But you can't leave well enough alone." Merrick's eyebrows were crowded together in the center of his face.

"Correct," Julia said. "One card, please."

There was silence while the men attended to the business of betting. Mayor Billy folded when Julia threw a dollar into the pot. Edgar Finnegan folded shortly after that. "I'll go see where the sandwiches are," he said, and stood up.

This left Julia playing with just Walt and Merrick.

Merrick tossed a two-bit piece into the center of the table. "Call," he said. And then, "What if we don't want to talk? What if we'd just like to play our usual quiet game of cards and not have to jabber with you about Hunter's business?"

"What about this?" she said, tossing her own two-bit piece into the pot.

"Fold," Walt said and leaned back in his chair. He rested his hands on his stomach and watched Merrick and Julia with a hint of mischief in his eyes and a smile flickering at the corners of his mouth.

"What if," Julia continued, "I only get to ask a question when I win a hand?"

Merrick looked up from his cards at her. "One question?"

"One question. Per hand won."

Merrick glanced at Walt and Billy, looking for their approval.

"Seems fair to me, Jack," the mayor said.

Merrick looked at Walt. The big Irishman said, "Fine with me. I'd let her stay regardless. She makes things interesting." He winked at Julia who smiled back at him.

Finnegan reentered the room carrying two large plates on one arm, piled high with Caroline's hand cut roast beef sandwiches. In his right hand he had a huge glass jar filled with pickles.

"Finn, Julia has a proposal," Merrick said to him. "For every round she wins she gets to ask a question about what we know about James Hunter."

Finnegan put the plates down on the side table and opened the jar of pickles. "Fine with me. It should be a pretty quiet night then." He stood up grinning and he too winked at Julia, showing her he meant no harm.

"Okay, then." Merrick looked uncharacteristically pleased with himself. Julia's stomach did a little flip. The cards she was holding were decent but the constable looked as though he believed he held the winning hand. Julia wasn't sure she could take the humiliation if she started losing. But she was in too deep now to back out.

"On that note," Merrick continued, "it's just down to you and me." He looked smug and confident and Julia had to admit she found the combination attractive. "Looks like you'll be quiet for a while yet." He laid his cards down on the table. "Straight," he said, and spread out a sequence of cards running from a four of clubs to an eight of hearts.

"Oh, dear," Julia said, "Well, that's too bad." She laid her cards down, "I only have a flush." She looked up and met Merrick's eyes. His face dropped in disappointment. "Oh, wait," she said, feigning ignorance, "a flush beats a straight, right? Silly me." She scooped the pot toward her.

"Ah, Merrick, she got ya," Finnegan clapped the constable on the back as he walked back to his chair. "You were bested by a wee lass."

AFTER THAT THINGS got tougher for Julia. The men were on their guard, which was too bad. She'd had more of an advantage when they thought nothing of her. And yet, she won her fair share of hands. Mayor Billy was an abysmal player and Finnegan wasn't that great either. They seemed to be in the game for the camaraderie and, in Mayor Billy's case, the food. He spent a great deal of time getting himself dealt out of hands so that he could stand at the sandwich table and crunch loudly on pickles.

"I swear to God," he said at one point, "if I didn't come to this game each week I'd starve to death." His round torso gave lie to this statement but none of the players challenged him.

At the end of the night, Julia suspected Walt of taking it easy on her. But Merrick did not. Most rounds went to one of them, although Finnegan did win a hand with a lucky deal. His poker face was terrible though and they all knew when he held an exceptional hand, and bowed out early. He didn't seem to care about the money and was just thrilled to win.

In the end Julia got six questions answered. This involved being dealt into eleven rounds and by the time that was over it was nearly midnight. She came away from the table several dollars richer, and, more to her satisfaction, a bit wealthier in information. She scooped her winnings into her purse and pulled on her gloves.

"Thank you so much, gentlemen. It's been my pleasure taking your money and your knowledge."

As she pulled the door closed behind her, she heard Mayor

Billy say, "Thank Christ that's over. I thought she'd never leave."

Julia poked her head back into the room, making the mayor jump, "Watch it, Mayor," she said, "Or next time I'll bring a certain wife of yours along."

CHAPTER FOURTEEN

T here was a set of stairs on the outside of the hotel that led down to the back door of the kitchen. Julia used them now, not wanting to use one of the main staircases that led into the restaurant and bar. Despite her bravado earlier, it would probably be wise not to be seen coming down from the hotel rooms at midnight by anyone.

Her purse was heavier than when she'd arrived, which sent a thrill through Julia's heart. She stepped down off the last stair onto the large yard behind the hotel. She intended to slip away into the night, hopefully remaining unseen, but she stopped short after a few steps. Voices were coming from inside the hotel kitchen; arguing and pleading. A man and a woman. Julia hesitated, and listened. She assumed Caroline Finnegan would step in and stop whatever was going on, but the longer Julia waited the more she realized that perhaps Caroline wasn't within earshot.

The woman's voice reached Julia's ears, "Alan, stop."

Julia took three steps and pulled open the kitchen's screened door.

Lily Cecil was standing beside the long table in the middle of the room. She was wearing her usual waitressing attire of dark dress with a white apron tied around her waist. Her corn silk hair was collected in a bun on the back of her head, but strands of it were falling loose. The kitchen had several lamps burning but it was still quite dark. Beside Lily was a man several inches taller than her. Julia couldn't see his face, as he had his back to her, but she could see he was slender, despite the bulk of the long waxed drover's coat he was wearing. He had his hat on, though he was inside; a black, wide-brimmed hat that reminded Julia of the one she wore when riding on sunny days.

The man had his left hand around Lily's upper arm. She was pulling away but he held fast. The look on Lily's face was one of mingled annoyance, fear and defiance.

"Excuse me," Julia said while the door closed behind her. "I'm looking for Mrs. Finnegan." The energy in the room was charged, like a building thunderstorm.

The man whirled around, startled. He let go of Lily's arm and looked Julia up and down with a quick flick of his eyes, a male habit that always annoyed her. There had been an angry expression on the man's face as he turned, but it was wiped away so quickly Julia almost thought she'd imagined it.

The man removed his hat. "Good evening, Miss Thom."

Julia wasn't sure how he knew her. "Good evening, Mr...?"

"Cecil. Alan Cecil. I'm Lily's husband." He smiled.

"Nice to meet you, Mr. Cecil. Hello Lily." Julia looked past the man. "You're working late tonight."

"Yes, Miss. I'm just finishing up and then Alan and I will head upstairs."

Julia remembered that Millie Jones had mentioned the Cecil's lived at the hotel. She met his eyes again.

"You weren't having a go at that poker game, were you?" Cecil grinned at her, his eyes sparkling now.

"I'm not sure I want to say, Mr. Cecil."

"Tell us now," Cecil leaned against the kitchen counter

and crossed one ankle over the other, "I'll bet you beat the pants off those guys, didn't you?"

All the hostility around Cecil and Lily was gone. The drover exuded warmth and friendliness. Julia felt herself slightly charmed by his relaxed attitude and roguish grin.

She smiled back at him. "As a matter of fact, I did."

Cecil laughed. "Ah! I knew it. You're a smart one, you are. You'd have to be to teach all those little rodents in your classroom. Can't have them getting one up on you, ever, right? They'd mutiny in an instant."

Julia chuckled, "What kind of a student were you, Mr. Cecil? I bet you caused a bit of trouble in your day."

"You're spot on, Miss Thom. I turned my teacher's hair white, I did. She was an old battle-ax though. A tough old bird." He laughed again, remembering, "We got up to lots of trouble, we did. Me and my mates. How do you keep your little ones in line with such a pretty face as you've got?"

Julia blushed slightly, unused to such blunt compliments. She was about to answer when Caroline Finnegan came through the swinging doors from the dining room.

"Lily!" She seemed surprised. "I thought you'd gone up ages ago."

"Just leaving now, Mrs. Finnegan. I was waiting for Alan."

"Right then. Off you go. See you tomorrow."

Lily untied her apron and shook it gently. She and Alan moved toward the back door and the staircase that Julia had just come down. "Good night," Lily said to Caroline. "Good night, Miss Thom."

Alan winked at Julia, "If you ever need any help keeping those wee beasties in line, Miss Thom, you let me know. I'll come and knock some sense into them."

"Thank you, Mr. Cecil. I will."

Julia nodded at the couple and then they were gone, the door flapping into the frame behind them. Caroline pulled off her apron and hung it on a hook where several others waited.

"I thought you'd gone too," she said to Julia. "Did you get what you wanted from those idiots?" She jerked her head toward the second floor, but used the word with fondness.

"I did," Julia answered. "And," she held her purse aloft and shook it, making the coins within jingle pleasantly, "I made a profit."

"Good for you!" Caroline seemed genuinely thrilled. "Spend it here, willya? We seem to be bleeding money at the moment."

"Really? This place is always busy."

"Aye, there may be bottoms in the seats at all hours, but no one can nurse a drink like this town's citizens. I should implement a three drink minimum or something."

Julia was sure Caroline was exaggerating. Other than a recently opened tea shop, that was mostly for ladies, Finnegan's restaurant was the only game in town if you wanted a meal other than one you'd cooked yourself. Not to mention the only place in town that served alcohol.

"How much of that money is Finn's?" Caroline asked, glancing at Julia's purse.

"A fair bit," Julia couldn't lie. "Your husband has a truly awful poker face."

Caroline sighed. "You are right about that. But you know the good news?"

"What?"

"The poor sod will never be able to cheat on me. I'd know it in a red hot second." She smiled broadly. "He gives himself away even when he takes an extra piece of pie."

CHAPTER FIFTEEN

J ulia was distracted the next day at school. Not to mention tired. She'd had trouble falling asleep once she was home. Thoughts about James Hunter and the information the men at the poker game had given her rolled around in her head, giving her what her mother called 'The Whirlies'. Finally, when she heard the clock in the living room strike a quarter past three, she began to drift off.

But morning had come too soon, and the children, picking up on her vulnerable state, had been restless and unable to focus themselves all day. She had taken them for a walk down to the lake to talk about marine life and erosion, a kind of impromptu science lesson, hoping the fresh air and exercise would settle them down a bit. But when they returned to the classroom to each write a story about what they'd seen or learned, they were more fidgety than ever. The weather had offered a little respite from the downward trend in temperatures, spiking to nearly fifty-nine degrees while they were out. This seemed to just emphasize to the children that they wanted to be outside, not in. She empathized with them; this would likely be the last really mild day until the spring. So finally at 2:30 she let them go. Their astonished little faces rewarded her. She would catch hell from some of the parents who would ask why she was being lenient, but that was fine. If there was one thing she'd learned since starting her job, it was that in the eyes of parents the teacher is nearly always at fault.

As she closed the door behind her and walked down the front steps, two boys were still playing in the yard, shooting at one another with sticks that stood in for revolvers.

Julia found Christopher Mitchell manning the store by himself.

"Good afternoon, Julia," he said when she pushed through the door, though his greeting lacked the usual enthusiasm he held for nearly everything.

"You look like you've lost your best friend, Christopher."

"I nearly have," he said, looking morose.

"What happened?" Julia was growing concerned.

"You'll have to ask my best friend. She's in the garden." He nodded his head in the direction of the back of the store.

Julia left without another word and walked behind the counter and outside through the storeroom.

She spotted Betty in the middle of the large patch of earth that was the store's garden. Growing season was over, but root vegetables and squash were still viable. Betty seemed to be pulling up carrots and beets. There was a large basket with a looped handle on the ground beside her. She angrily tossed a carrot into it as Julia approached.

"Your husband is in the doghouse, I take it," Julia said as she approached.

Betty stood up straight, a slightly startled look in her eye. "Oh, Julia. I didn't hear you sneaking up on me."

"I wasn't sneaking. You were preoccupied."

She turned back and bent toward the dirt again. "Perhaps."

Julia had no experience being married, but she knew a

marital spat when she saw one. Her parents were both strong-willed and stubborn people. Julia inherited her best qualities - tenacity, intelligence and a self-assuredness from them. And it was also the place where she gleaned her worst characteristics, including the stubbornness that was beginning to be the largest irritant for Constable Merrick. Julia never mediated with her parents, even as she got older. She didn't feel it was her place to do so, plus she knew she would almost invariably side with her father, who was her best friend. Julia and her mother were too close in temperament to be anything but adversaries, and by the time Julia was about ten years old, they'd forged a mutual silent agreement to leave each other alone.

So Julia didn't feel equipped or inclined to step into whatever was causing disharmony in the Mitchell household. However, what she did know was that Betty Mitchell was her closest friend, and someone she could trust and rely on, even though they'd known each other for less than two months. Betty and Christopher were both good people and even this early on, Julia would have done almost anything for either of them. So she said the one thing her Aunt Ruby used to say when Julia was bent out of shape about something. It was the best thing anyone had ever said to her in such circumstances and it came to her now, though she had not seen or spoken to her Aunt in several years.

"Tell me about it," Julia said, and she tried to adopt the neutral and compassionate tone Aunt Ruby used.

"Oh, Julia," Betty threw another carrot violently into the basket. It bounced off the basket's rim and landed in the dirt. "Christopher is trying to bankrupt us. He's practically given away the store."

"What? How?"

"Maybe not the store." Betty backpedaled a bit. "But most of the inventory." She looked away toward the hills to the west that bordered the town, tears glistening in her eyes. "You know what a soft heart he has. He lets people run up credit and never asks them to pay. Now that we've been here nearly a year, people are learning to take advantage of him. And word gets around."

Julia touched her friend's arm in sympathy.

Betty continued, "Yesterday, when I was in the back making lunch he had a rancher in here who is new to the area. This fellow ran up forty dollars of credit. Christopher had never met the man before!" She threw her hands up in the air in a gesture of frustration. "We'll probably never see the man again, so Christopher essentially gave him two months of supplies. Forty dollars!"

"Oh, dear."

"And the worst part of it is, he knows it's the wrong thing to do. He feels bad about it afterward and then he hides what he's done. He hides the credit slips and I've had no idea how bad the situation is. But in the moment, his soft heart gets the better of him, and he just offers to help out any Joe who comes into the store."

"He's embarrassed that people are taking advantage of him."

"Damn right he is." Julia had never heard Betty swear before. She tucked her chin into her neck to hide her smile. "And he should be. Do you know how much credit he's extended in the past eight months?"

Julia shook her head.

Betty's eyes filled with tears and then spilled over. Her chin shook. She said, almost whispering, "Nearly five hundred dollars."

The figure rocked Julia back. It was an enormous amount of money. No wonder Betty was worried. Julia wasn't sure what to say. This was far worse than she imagined. She reached into her purse and brought out a handkerchief to hand to her friend.

Betty plowed on. "All the credit slips were hidden in a box

at the back of a shelf under the counter. This morning I was searching for the scraps of a bolt of fabric that I thought I'd kept for quilting and I came across this box I'd never seen before. It was filled with credit slips." She looked off into the distance again and Julia could see the fear and sense of betrayal on her friend's face. "Nearly five hundred dollars. How are we ever going to recover from that?"

The world was quiet while Betty thought about this. Finally she spoke up again. "And how will I ever trust him again?"

THE TWO WOMEN didn't come up with a solution, standing there in the yard. After sharing her tale of woe for a while longer, Betty eventually ran out of steam.

"Come upstairs. Let's have some tea and talk about something else."

The Mitchells lived above their store in a suite of rooms that included a kitchen, living area and two large bedrooms, one at the front of the building and one at the back. They had built the building when they'd moved to Horse and had lived at the Finnegan's hotel the previous spring and summer while it was being built. The furniture was sparse but well cared for, and the rooms had a cozy, welcoming feel. It was strange to Julia to be one story off the ground but she enjoyed the view from the sitting room windows, which looked out across Lake Okanagan. The lakefront was a few blocks away, but the water still glinted and sparkled in the afternoon sunlight.

The routine of making and serving tea seemed to calm Betty. Tears had stopped leaking from her eyes and she looked slightly less shattered than she had when Julia first found her in the garden. The carrots and beets were left in their basket on the back porch, and the women climbed the set of stairs that went up on the outside of the building.

When they were settled with tea and biscuits, Betty said,

"You didn't come over here just to counsel me, I'm sure, Julia. Were you looking for something?"

"Now that you ask, I wanted to talk to you about James Hunter's beating."

"Oh, good!" Betty took a bite of her goodie, "Please take my mind off ..." she paused, "well, everything."

"I went to the hotel last night in search of information."

"Did you? What sort of information?"

"Let me back up. Yesterday afternoon, Earnest Hewitt came by the school to pick up his son and his neighbor's son. He does that sometimes. Out of nowhere, he mentioned a poker game that takes place each week."

Betty's eyes widened.

"Did you know about this?"

The storekeeper shook her head.

"Me, neither. And Mr. Hewitt didn't say where it was. I was so shocked and he drove off before I could ask him any more questions. So I asked the Engs..."

"Who know everything," Betty chimed in.

Julia nodded. "And they eventually told me it was at the hotel. Anyway, with a little persuasion Caroline Finnegan told me which room it was in and I went and played a few hands."

"You did not!"

"I did."

"Julia Thom, you scandalous hussie."

"Why, thank you." Julia smiled, pleased with the effect her story was having. Some of the light returned to Betty's eyes. "I wanted to find out if James Hunter owed anyone money or had annoyed anyone there. He's completely clammed up and won't talk to Merrick or anyone about what happened to him. But I'm determined to find the culprit who did this to him."

"So what did they say?"

"Hewitt had said that Hunter was a poor player, and they liked having him at the game for that reason. He always had a lot of cash with him and was good at sharing it with the other players, if you get my meaning."

Betty took a sip of tea and nodded.

"It took some persuasion but I was able to get Merrick and Walt and Finn to confirm this. Hunter was a terrible player, they said. But that wouldn't cause anyone to beat him up. Quite the opposite, in fact. They liked having him there. He was quiet and caused no trouble."

"Oh," Betty sat back slightly in her chair. "So you're not any closer to finding out who attacked him?

"I didn't say that," Julia said.

"Do tell."

"Well," Julia was relishing sharing the story. She'd been sitting on it all day. "Apparently, despite Mr. Hunter's tendency toward being quiet and minding his own business, he and Roy Meddy got into an argument at last week's game."

"Roy Meddy is a right bastard."

Julia barked out a sharp burst of laughter at Betty's choice phrase. This was more swearing than Betty had done the entire time Julia had known her. She liked this new, angry Betty Mitchell.

"It's true," Betty laughed along with Julia. "For a man whose business is making sweets, he's as sour as they come. That poor wife of his."

"Exactly! Now, here's my question for you. I thought that I overheard someone say that Roy was violent and had beaten his wife on more than one occasion."

Betty set down her teacup and thought about this. "I've heard that rumor too, but I'm not sure how true it is. I've never seen evidence of anything like that. Although some people are better at hiding that sort of thing. But he is a bastard, like I said, and always has to have his own way. Everyone knows that. He can't stand being wrong or even being unsure about something. Plus he's always got his nose in everyone's business. In fact, I stopped dealing with him. We used to stock a few loaves of bread here in the shop. Meddy would bring them over each morning when we were opening up and sell them to us at cost. But we never knew how many he'd bring and if we asked him to commit he'd get all fractious with us. I stopped dealing with him altogether because he was so rude to me. I left him for Christopher to manage. But even he got fed up with Meddy's behavior eventually. So we stopped carrying the bread." Betty thought for a few minutes, staring out the window. "He does make an amazing apple tart, though. I'll give him that."

"Well," Julia took a last sip of tea and began pulling her gloves on, "he's the closest thing I've got to a suspect, so I'm going over there now to see what I can find out. Maybe he'll confess and that will be that."

"Is Constable Merrick going with you?"

Julia shook her head. "I am doing this without his approval, although probably not without his knowledge. He's busy trying to find the men who tried to attack me last Saturday night."

Betty shivered. "Deputize me then, and I'll come with you."

"Deputize you?" Julia looked at Betty quizzically. "I'm not a police officer. I'm not a deputy myself. Merrick would chew off his own left foot before he'd involve me officially in a case."

"Go on. Wave your hands in the air or cast a magic spell, or whatever. Make me a deputy."

Never in her life had Julia had a woman friend who understood her the way Betty did. Her heart swelled. She stood up. "Betty Mitchell, I do hereby declare that you are henceforth and furthermore my deputy. Amen. Or something."

Betty grinned and stood up as well. "I live to serve."

CHAPTER SIXTEEN

Is there anything more enticing than the smell of warm bread? Julia's mouth began to water before she and Betty even entered Meddy's shop. The smell reminded Julia of home, and of Ella, the Thom's cook, who always let Julia help with the kneading and would use a tiny bit of dough to make her a very small bun. It was their secret and as far as Julia knew her mother never found out. When the baking was done, Ella and Julia would sit at the small table in the kitchen, a pot of tea between them. Julia would eat her bun with one ear listening for footsteps in the hallway in case her mother should make a surprise appearance. She rarely did. The kitchen was a realm she preferred to leave to others' care.

Meddy's shop was tucked into a strange spot on Main Street. The lot where it stood had, for whatever reason, been assigned a smaller width than all the others on the street. Consequently the bakery always looked squished to Julia, like it was a theater-goer in tight seats, holding in its shoulders. Meddy, on the other hand, was not burdened with a lack of spread. He was thick everywhere; thick neck, thick midsection, thick fingers. And a thick head, Julia's father would have said, but she had thus far tried to give the man the benefit of the doubt.

Today, however, he would have to prove himself to her. She was convinced he was the likeliest suspect for Hunter's beating. He had the means (his ham shaped hands and quick temper) and the motive (his argument with Hunter at the previous week's poker game). Whether he had the opportunity would remain to be seen. Could he account for his whereabouts on Monday? Julia found Hunter just after 3:30pm, but who knew how long he'd been lying on the floor of his shop. The Meddys tended to close up shop as soon as they'd sold out of everything, which was usually by 2pm. They lived in a house several blocks away and were rarely seen in the afternoons and evenings. They woke early, long before daylight, year round, to start baking, and went to bed early as well, to facilitate this.

Julia and Betty's discussion hadn't begun until mid-afternoon and now it was nearly four o'clock. Julia was surprised to find the Meddys still in their shop. The baskets that lined the shelves in the shop were nearly empty, though there were a few loaves left. Julia assumed this was what was causing the late opening.

"Good afternoon, Mr. Meddy," she said brightly, feigning delight at seeing the baker. "Thank goodness you've got some bread left!" Julia eyed the baskets beside her. None of the bread was her favorite and, in fact, she'd just made a loaf for herself on Sunday.

"You left it a bit late, didn't ya?" Meddy asked, hardly looking up from where he was sweeping flour dust and grains into a pile.

Charmer, Julia thought. "I'll take this last loaf of rye," she said, "and Mrs. Mitchell will have these last two loaves of sourdough." Julia jabbed her friend gently in the ribs.

Betty startled but she recovered quickly. "Yes please, Mr. Meddy. And Julia will be paying for everything today."

Touché, Julia thought.

With great ill nature, Meddy put the loaves into the basket Betty had the foresight to bring with her. Then he acted like he was doing Julia a favor taking her payment.

When the women stayed where they were, rather than turning and leaving the shop, Meddy glared at them both and asked, "That it?"

"Now that you mention it, we have a question for you," Julia said.

"We?" Betty muttered under her breath.

"What is it?" Meddy barked.

"You're an acquaintance of Mr. Hunter, the watchmaker, aren't you?" Julia led with an easy question but Meddy wasn't ready to take the bait.

"Not really, no. Can't say I am."

Julia played one of her best cards; a little early she reflected later, but then, she was new at the suspect interview game. "You see him each week at the poker game at Finnegan's though, correct?"

Meddy hardly reacted at all to this revelation. If Julia hadn't been watching closely she would have missed the slight movement backwards of his head. "Who says?" he countered.

"Well, let's see," Julia pretended for a moment that her bow was empty and then loosed a surprise arrow. "Constable Merrick, Mayor Billy, Walt Sheehan and Edgar Finnegan for a start."

This time Meddy had prepared himself. He didn't flinch. "Is that right? And what have they got to say about this theoretical poker game?"

Two points to you for the use of 'theoretical', Julia thought. Perhaps she had underestimated the size of the brain encased behind Meddy's porcine eyes and ill humor. "One thing they said last night when I was playing with them," she paused for effect, "was that last week you had quite a disagreement with Mr. Hunter. You accused him of cheating."

Julia raised her voice a little in triumph which caused Meddy to glance back toward the back door of the shop.

"Keep your voice down, woman," Meddy said. Clearly Mrs. Meddy wasn't aware of her husband's participation in the game.

Julia made a mental note and filed it for later.

Meddy continued, at a hissed whisper. "You're goddamned right I accused that little weasel of cheating. He rarely wins and then suddenly he had a night when he couldn't lose. How is that possible? I told him I would break all his limbs if I ever figured out how he was doing it."

"Doing what?"

"Cheating, of course!" Meddy looked at Julia as though she was an imbecile.

"And did you?"

Now Meddy looked puzzled. "Did I what?"

"Did you try to break all his limbs?"

"I wish I had," Meddy hissed. "That little turd deserves whatever he got. Keeps hisself to hisself and then flounces into the game and fleeces us all. Smarmy little bastard. I'll figure out how he did it one day. And then he *will* receive a beating. You mark my words." He paused slightly, perhaps suddenly aware of what he'd just said. "But no," he eventually continued, "I didn't touch him this time. And I got no idea who did."

"Are you sure, Mr. Meddy? Edgar Finnegan said he and Walt Sheehan had to remove you from last week's game because you were so enraged at Mr. Hunter. It would have been so easy to find him at his shop, all alone, and give him what you thought he deserved. I'm sure you were justified if Hunter was cheating." Julia was laying it on thick now, trying to get Meddy to admit his wrongdoing.

But Meddy was having none of it. "If I had figured out how he'd cheated I'da beat him for sure and taken whatever punishment was coming to me. Finnegan and Sheehan threw me out and I had time to cool off. I'm choosing to bide my time and get to the bottom of whatever that little rat is doing. I want that useless tit, Merrick, to know. He refused to get involved last week. Wouldn't hear what I had to say. I'll show them all when Hunter comes back to the table and I figure it out."

He sounded adamant. Julia didn't know the man well enough to tell if he was lying. He was a bully and in her experience bullies often made up their stories to fit their victimized version of things. She decided to approach from another angle. "Where were you on Monday afternoon, Mr. Meddy?"

"Where the hell do you think I was, lass? Right where you see me now. We don't get..."

The back door of the shop opened and closed. Meddy snapped to attention. "Thank you ladies," he said loudly, "enjoy your bread. The missus and me will be heading home now." He put an arm each behind Julia and Betty and ushered them in no uncertain terms toward the front door. Before they knew it they were out on the street and the door was closing and latching behind them. Betty still had her basket over one arm.

"Two loaves of sourdough?" she asked her friend. "What on earth am I going to do with them?"

"Sell them," Julia suggested, "and make back some of the cash you need to cover the debts your husband is owed."

"And make what? A penny each?"

"Every penny counts, as my old gran used to say."

CHAPTER SEVENTEEN

"Do you think a woman could have inflicted that harm on Mr. Hunter?"

Julia was sitting in Dr. Parker's office. He was a man of few words. He reminded Julia of Walt Sheehan in that way, except it was different with Parker. There was a tightness about him, like something coiled. Where Walt was quiet because he was observing and accepting everything around him, Parker seemed always to be restraining himself, holding back somehow. Julia imagined that being the only doctor in town couldn't be easy. Much like Constable Merrick's job, she thought the doctoring position in Horse might be a lonely one. Parker was unmarried and Julia guessed him to be about fifty years old. She didn't know if he had been married at some point. She had never been in a social situation with the man so that she could ask him more about himself. She suspected he preferred it that way.

He had an impressive mustache that was greyer than the hair on his head. It floated down over his upper lip and made Julia's own lips tickle just looking at it. He often looked tired, she thought, and his expression was stern, which went along with his personality. He kept his hair cut quite short, much shorter than most men. His hands were always clean, the nails trimmed right back. He had thickened through the middle with age, and occasionally seemed self-conscious about that, covering his belly with his hands.

He was thinking about her question, leaning back in his chair, which tilted on its base when he did so. The walls around her were gleaming white and the sunlight coming through the windows caught in the glass jars around the room and made them sparkle.

Julia waited, knowing enough not to rush the man.

Parker came forward on his chair and laid his hands on his desk. "He's not talking?"

"No. He won't speak to Constable Merrick. He says he doesn't remember anything about the attack."

"Why are you asking?" Parker placed the emphasis on the word 'you', highlighting that Julia was not officially employed to ask such questions.

She straightened her spine. "I want to help. Merrick is swamped with other work and Hunter isn't able to provide him with any information. I thought I'd do a little digging and see if I can put the pieces together."

Parker watched her with a calm detachment that she found unnerving. "Does Merrick approve?"

"No."

For the first time a faint smile touched Parker's lips. "I expect not. Well..." he nodded, thinking again. "I can't say too much. Doctor-patient confidentiality and all that. But since you saw Hunter's injuries yourself I can speak to those. My assessment is that most of the injuries were not inflicted by a weapon."

This didn't surprise Julia. Until now she had been operating on the premise that it was fists that had caused the bruising and wounds on Hunter's face.

"What about his broken arm?"

"He could have fallen on it during the attack. The break is

low down on his arm. Almost at his wrist. That tells me it could be the result of an impact."

"Like landing on it."

"Yes, like that. Land on it at the wrong angle and the bone snaps under the weight being forced down on it. He's not a big man but when we fall, of course, our weight is multiplied by the force of the fall."

Julia sat quietly for a moment, thinking.

Parker surprised her by volunteering some information. "Fists, well, knuckles really, break the skin on impact. Hunter had that head wound, which may have been caused by knocking it against something. But the bruising around his face was mostly just that - bruising. There wasn't much broken skin, except that cut on his lip."

"But there's no way to tell," Julia said, coming back to her original question, "if the wounds could have been inflicted by a woman."

Parker shook his head.

"Why wouldn't he have defended himself?" Julia was thinking out loud. "If it was a woman he could theoretically have grabbed her arms to restrain her."

"Maybe it was a surprise attack."

"Still. Who wouldn't try to stop someone who was battering them?"

The doctor looked out the window, thinking. When he turned back to Julia she could see he had made a decision. "When I removed his shirt and vest, there was quite a bit of bruising and redness here." He held up his own left arm and pointed with his right hand to the underside of the forearm, between elbow and wrist. "On both arms."

Parker then waited while Julia processed that information. "Defensive wounds," she said.

Parker nodded. "That's what I thought." He held both his arms up in front of his face. "If he was shielding himself, like this, it's that part of the arm that would take most of the force of the blows. And it's a very natural, human instinct to protect one's face and eyes in such an event." He put his hands back down on the desk. "Why do you ask about whether a woman could have done the damage?"

"Just a suspicion I have based on a conversation I had with someone this morning."

JULIA MADE it a habit to stop in to see James Hunter each morning on her way to school. Betty, Millie Jones and several other women in town were keeping him stocked with food. The man had probably never eaten so well. His suits might not fit when he was ready to go back to work. The women always stayed for a visit when they dropped off a stew or soup, although Betty mentioned that Hunter never wanted to chat for long. He always seemed relieved when she took her leave. Julia had the same experience each morning. She wanted to make sure Hunter had had a good rest and was set up with tea and whatever breakfast he might want. He never asked her to do anything extra and she wondered if he even ate the porridge she made him.

This morning as she had approached the house, she'd heard shouting from inside. It almost sounded like two female voices. Julia broke into a run and dashed up the front walk. The front door was not quite closed and she could identify Lily Cecil's voice as she pushed through.

"Mr. Hunter? Is everything all right?"

Hunter was standing in front of one of the upholstered chairs in his parlor. Lily was standing several feet away. Both were red in the face. Hunter was dressed for the first time since he'd come home from Dr. Parker's. His suit jacket was slung over his right shoulder so that his broken arm could rest in the sling. Julia fleetingly wondered how he'd managed to get dressed and put the sling on.

Lily and Hunter abruptly stopped arguing the instant they

saw Julia come through the door. Their jaws snapped shut and the room was suddenly filled with uneasy silence. Julia felt like a child who had interrupted a parental argument.

She said again, "Is everything all right?"

Hunter and Lily looked at one another and then Hunter assured Julia, "Yes. Everything is fine, Miss Thom. Lily, er, Mrs. Cecil and I were just having a disagreement about whether I should go back to work today."

"You're not thinking of going back to work yet, are you?"

Hunter nodded, decisively, "I am. Today. I can't sit around here any longer. I've got customers waiting."

"But Mr. Hunter, you only have the use of one arm."

"Then I'll be slow. But I must go back. If I stay here staring at the walls for one more minute I'll go mad."

Julia didn't know what to say. The man was captain of his own ship and she had no authority over him. She looked at the other woman, "You must feel it would be better if he rested for a few more days?"

Lily looked confused for a moment. Julia was starting to feel she wasn't the smartest of women. She glanced at Hunter and then she said, "Yes. Yes, that's right. I think a few more days of rest are in order."

Lily had taken her leave then, bidding them both good day and walking through the front door that was still hanging open. Hunter watched her go with an expression in his eyes that Julia couldn't identify.

Julia helped Hunter finish getting dressed and then walked the man to his shop. He was even quieter than usual, which hardly seemed possible. Julia wondered if he was really feeling well enough to spend a day at his shop.

He unlocked the door and they stepped inside together.

"Well," Julia said, "you can always go home and rest anytime you need to. Your customers will understand."

Hunter nodded absently, not really seeming to hear her. He was surveying the spots of blood on the floor behind the counter. "That's the first thing I'll need to clean up, isn't it?" he said. "Can't have customers walking into a watchmaker's and thinking they're in a butcher's shop."

This was the first time Julia had ever heard Hunter make what could be construed as a joke. She smiled at him and noticed the bruises around his eyes were turning quite a foul shade of green. "Let me help you with that," she said, beginning to pull off her gloves.

"No, Miss Thom," Hunter put one of his slight hands on her arm and then pulled it away quickly, "You've done enough. I thank you. You're going to be late for school. I've got all day to tidy up around here, so that's just what I'm going to do. You go now." He pulled his mouth into a faint smile.

"I'll check in on you on my way home this afternoon."

"That would be kind of you."

Julia walked to school slowly, mulling over what had just unfolded. The tension between Hunter and Lily seemed odd to her. It had a familiarity about it, the way that she had observed siblings can be with one another. Lily had said to Julia that she had known Mr. Hunter at school, but she hadn't mentioned when they'd last seen one another before they both moved to Horse. And, in the moment, Julia hadn't thought to ask. You have to know someone well enough to argue with them. This trail of thoughts caused Julia to wonder if Lily and Hunter had a broken engagement that they didn't want talked about. People did so often hide the truth, especially when it involved protecting personal business.

When it came to living in a small town, in a place as far from anywhere as Horse was, one almost had to be running from something. Many in town and the surrounding area, of course, were running toward something; a better future, a different life. But Julia knew intimately that many people, including herself, were trying to leave a past behind them. She wondered if James Hunter was one of these. She determined to go and talk to Dr. Parker when school was finished for the afternoon.

Her thoughts were interrupted when Susan and Ellen, her two grade-six students, came running down the street toward her.

"Good morning, ladies," Julia said, putting aside her circling thoughts about past connections and present troubles.

The girls flung themselves at their teacher, braids bouncing, speaking over one another indecipherably.

"Slow down, girls. Slow down. What are you saying?"

Ellen Simcoe, self-proclaimed den mother of all the children younger than herself, put her hands on her hips and declared, "Peter Little was eating dirt, Miss Thom, and now he's thrown up on his shoes."

Julia almost burst out laughing. This was an unexpected benefit of working with children that she hadn't anticipated when she'd applied for the job. One moment was always vastly different from its predecessor. She could never predict what each day would hold and she loved that. Children brought a unique brand of beautiful chaos that she hadn't realized she'd been missing from her life.

"Well then, nurses, lead on," she said. "Take me to your patient."

PETER LITTLE's dirt-eating escapades aside, it was a quiet and thankfully smooth day at school. Julia found Dr. Parker in his office immediately after she closed the school for the day. And although he was willing to talk to her, the conversation left Julia feeling more confused than anything.

James Hunter seemed to be an enigma. Everyone knew of him, but no one seemed to know him. She knew him as well to be a man who was stand-offish and remote. Almost like he always had somewhere to go, some place to be other than talking to the person he was with at that moment. She experienced this feeling even when she and Betty were in his home, helping him with the cooking and cleaning. He never seemed entirely relaxed.

How could someone so difficult to reach have created an enemy who despised him so much he would beat the man half to death? Hunter was a puff of smoke. A ghost. Who could he have offended so badly?

And furthermore, why didn't he want to talk about it? This was the part that really stuck in Julia's mind. He claimed he remembered nothing from the attack, not one shred of any part of the event had stayed with him. She found this very hard to believe. Was he covering something up? Was the beating somehow tied into something illegal or immoral? Julia found that just as hard to believe. A woman in 1890 had to be keenly aware of the character of those around her. Julia knew that she wasn't the only woman who had developed a sixth sense about those men she could trust and those she couldn't. Even before moving to Horse this skill was something she had mastered. Her mother had insisted on it and some of their only meaningful conversations, at least the ones that weren't about how to steep tea and what constituted proper attire for a Tuesday afternoon cello concert, had been about this subject. Julia often wondered if her mother had been hurt in some way when she was younger. But it was a subject she had never broached. She wouldn't have known how.

James Hunter was not someone who ever struck Julia as being dangerous. And that he came to her aid at the dance showed that he was willing to stick his neck out for others. He cared about Julia's well-being that night, though he had gone back into his shell immediately afterward.

As Julia walked away from the school, thinking hard about all this, she remembered that the gun Hunter had pointed at her assailants had surprised her on the night of the dance. She knew no one except Constable Merrick who owned a handgun. Most people, including herself, owned a rifle or a shot-gun. She kept a rifle in the scabbard of her saddle in case she needed to deal with a wild animal while out riding. Although Walt Sheehan teased her and said that it was really just a pea-shooter that would only annoy a bear or a mountain lion should she encounter one. But it made her feel safer when riding on her own. When she remembered to take it.

And most, if not all, families had a similar weapon. Not in the city perhaps, but definitely in small towns like Horse. Guns were used to shoot the game that provided most of the meat a family would consume during the year. All the boys in Julia's class who were over the age of ten had a small rifle of their own. Fathers taught sons how to hunt; it was just part of keeping a family well-fed.

But handguns, revolvers, were another story. Julia had hardly ever seen one in person until the night Hunter came to her aid. Merrick wore his at his side in a leather holster, but it hung underneath his suit jacket and Julia rarely thought about it.

Julia's walk slowed as she continued to think. Owning a handgun was perhaps one thing, but why would Hunter have it with him while he was out for a walk? That in itself was completely puzzling and something she decided she needed to talk to Hunter about. Her pace picked up again. She had a plan, though the longer she pursued the question of who had beaten Hunter, the more puzzled she became. It was absurd, in a way, to be trying to solve a crime that the victim seemed to want to ignore. *Ah well*, she thought, *it's not the first time I've done something without someone's permission.*

CHAPTER EIGHTEEN

For the second time in as many weeks, the schoolhouse was being used for a town event. This time, it was the harvest potluck lunch.

After church on Sunday, Pastor Thoreson was gently but firmly ushered out of the building so that his wife and the other women could set up the room. There was to be a pie contest, which the pastor was to officiate. "You can't see the ladies arriving with their pies, Harry," Mrs. Thoreson said, practically pushing him down the stairs. "It needs to be an impartial contest."

"You know I would know your pie anywhere, Anne," her husband said, kissing her on the cheek.

"Well, good thing I'm not entering the contest then. Now get along. There's bread, cheese and pickle for your lunch. But don't eat too much. Leave room for pie. And come back in an hour."

Anne Thoreson was a tiny woman. If she topped five feet Julia would have been surprised. But this tiny package came with a tremendous amount of energy. Julia didn't think she'd ever seen Mrs. Thoreson sitting down, except at church. The Thoresons came from back east, reassigned from Ottawa, Julia seemed to recall, and in Horse there was never enough for Mrs. Thoreson to do. She was part of, or ran, every committee the town had. She raised money for missionaries in Africa. She quilted like a dream and had gifted almost everyone in town with a quilt at one time or another. The one she had given Julia was a double wedding-ring pattern. "For good luck, dear," Mrs. Thoreson had said, which almost made Julia laugh.

The Thoresons had been blessed with two boys, but, tragically, both had been killed in an accident long before the pastor and his wife moved to Horse. "They fell through the ice on a lake there in Ontario," Millie Jones whispered to Julia one day as they left church together. "They were twelve and fourteen. So sad." Millie had tisk-tisked and Julia was struck by how people managed to keep putting one foot in front of the other after such an event. How was it possible? But there the Thoresons were, intact and seemingly happy, though the sorrow of their loss had surely never left them. Even so, they acted like love birds with one another. Julia had yet to have an encounter with them when they didn't touch one another. If Julia had seen her parents touch twice in her lifetime she'd be surprised.

When she was sure her husband was out of sight, Mrs. Thoreson came back into the schoolhouse and began organizing the buffet tables and chairs, as well as the places of honor for the judges of the pie tasting contest. Julia and Betty were there to work, and Mrs. Thoreson didn't hold back assigning them tasks to do. By the time the room began filling up with families and couples, Julia felt a little damp under her arms, which made her self-conscious. Her mother would not approve of a woman of Julia's position doing anything other than sitting on the sidelines and looking pretty. Despite the sticky underarm situation, Julia liked that her life now would shock her mother in so many ways.

Tables were set up around the perimeter of the room, and

as guests arrived they added their dishes and pots of stew to the bounty. Everyone brought their own bowl or plate and filled these to the brim. Smaller tables had been set up around the room, each with three or four chairs. At an event like this, those who lived closest to the schoolhouse brought their dining table and chairs so that they could be used.

Soon the schoolroom was groaning under the weight of the people, the tables, and the food laid out. The volume rose several decibels every few minutes. Children, dressed in their Sunday best, ran through the forest of legs, their energy crackling with excitement.

This was a daytime event and, as such, there was no music. Julia spied Jack Merrick on the far side of the room, standing alone, his back to a wall. She took pity on him and brought him a bottle of Mayor Jones' cider.

"Have you tried this, Constable?" She held the bottle out toward him.

He raised his right arm and showed her a bottle already in his right hand.

"Ah, okay then." Julia hesitated, while Merrick watched her. He had a way of looking at her in some moments that made her decidedly uncomfortable; the way a cat watches birds from behind glass. It was the first time they had spoken since the poker game and Julia remembered how unhappy he'd seemed about her presence. She felt that perhaps he didn't want to talk to her now, so she began to turn away.

Then Merrick said something she didn't catch.

"Pardon me?" she turned back.

"Why don't you have it?" There was a change in his expression. He was almost arching one eyebrow.

It was a challenge. Women didn't drink alcohol in public.

He must have seen the internal struggle she was having. "If anyone asks, I'll say it's mine," he offered.

Now she couldn't back down. Annoyed with herself for being so easily coerced, she opened the bottle, pulling the stopper out, and took a surreptitious swig, turning her body so that Merrick shielded her from most of the room. The cider was sweet and a little tingly on her tongue. It tasted very pleasant, although strong. Her eyes lit up.

"It's nice, isn't it?" Merrick smiled at her.

"It's a hell of a lot better than that awful grog Walt makes, that's for sure."

"Aye. That stuff will have you breathing fire in no time."

"Where is the blacksmith, anyway?"

"He's on his way. Nelson threw a shoe this morning when we were out, so he wanted to see to that before he came over. He won't miss the pie though. Don't worry."

Julia wasn't worried and wasn't sure why Merrick used the phrase, but she pushed the thought aside and asked, "When were you out? Before church?"

"Aye."

"You must've been up before the sun."

"We were."

Julia could tell if she wanted any details from Merrick she was going to have to ask for them. "Pleasure trip?" she said, casually.

"Nope. Business."

Julia waited and seethed slightly, her curiosity battling with her unwillingness to let Merrick think he had the upper hand.

He watched her for a moment and then took pity on her. "We went out to the Piling place. I wanted to talk to the drovers out there, and Walt wanted to come along for some fresh air."

Julia realized now why Merrick had been reluctant to tell her where he'd been; he hadn't wanted her to go with him as she had to the Double A Ranch. She was wondering how to phrase her next question when he offered more.

"No one suspicious there. None of Piling's drovers come into town much. He doesn't pay them enough. Besides, two of them limp. One from a foot he broke recently falling off his horse, and the other from an old knee injury. You didn't notice your two fellows limping did you? You would have told me that."

Julia didn't like Merrick calling them 'her fellows' but she let it pass. Her mind brought up an image from the night of the dance, the men walking on either side of her. "No," she said, "I'm certain neither of them limped."

Walt joined them then, coming in from outside smelling of fresh air and earth, and Julia was grateful for the distraction. His hair was slicked down with water and he had on a clean shirt and a vest and jacket she hadn't seen before. "You look all spiffed up, Mr. Sheehan."

Walt grunted and glanced around the room. "Anything to drink around here?"

"Here," Julia said, thrusting the bottle of cider into his hands, grateful for an excuse to be rid of it. The cider was pleasant, but she really didn't need any reason for the town to consider her a woman of loose morals.

Walt nodded to her and took the bottle, tipping it back and drinking at least half in one long pull. "Ah," he said, wiping his mouth on his hand, "that's the stuff."

Anne Thoreson appeared out of nowhere at Julia's elbow. "Constable Merrick, I must pull you away now. We're ready to begin the pie tasting."

"You're a judge?" Julia and Walt said to Merrick simultaneously.

"Don't knock it," Merrick said as Mrs. Thoreson pulled him away.

"He'll be sorry if he doesn't pick wee Mrs. Jones' pie," Walt said under his breath. He always called Millie 'wee Mrs. Jones', even to her face. She loved it and blushed like a schoolgirl, not realizing he was being ironic.

· · ·

117

For Julia, the rest of the afternoon passed in a whirl of conversation and good food. The volume in the room crept up until it was nearly impossible to talk to anyone without shouting. But she was having a wonderful time. She got to meet several couples from ranches around the town who she had not encountered until that day. Betty and Christopher seemed to be patching things up; at least they were talking to one another again, though if that was only for public consumption, Julia couldn't be sure. And it was Betty's strawberry-rhubarb pie that won the contest. Julia didn't even know her friend had entered. Although in hindsight, it wasn't entirely surprising. Hers was the best pie Julia had ever tasted, better even than Ella the Cook's at home.

Lily Cecil had entered the contest as well, with the apple pie she so often made for the hotel restaurant. She came in third. Alan Cecil happened to be standing near Julia when the winners were announced. Lily accepted her prize of a new pie plate and approached her husband. Julia congratulated her as she went past.

"Thank you, Miss Thom," Lily said.

"You should be proud of yourself." Julia thought the young woman looked quite disappointed and tried to cheer her up. "You came in ahead of four other ladies."

"You're right," Lilly nodded, but she didn't look as though she agreed with Julia.

As Lily reached her husband, Julia heard him say, "That was a surprise. I didn't expect you to even make the top five."

Julia's eyes flared at this, but she forced herself to bite her tongue. She turned away and found Gerald Anker and a woman approaching her.

"Miss Thom. Have you met my wife?" Anker said.

Julia and the woman nodded at one another.

Anker continued, "Sabine, this is Miss Thom, the school-teacher."

Mrs. Anker was a petite woman with small features and a

serious expression. And, it turned out, a thick German accent. "Pleased to be meeting you Miss Thom," she said. "Did you have a pie in the contest?"

"No, did you?"

Mrs. Anker shook her head. "No, I'm a terrible baker."

"Now, dear, your bread is delicious," Anker said, smiling at his wife with indulgence.

She patted his arm with a gloved hand, "You're being generous, mein Bärchen. It is not a skill I've perfected, Miss Thom. I'd rather be sewing. The kitchen does not interest me."

"Amen," Julia said, making Mrs. Anker laugh.

"Did you get a pumpkin, Miss Thom?" Anker asked her.

"A pumpkin?"

"We've brought one for everyone," the red-faced man clasped his hands behind his back and rolled on the balls of his feet. "Our crop was generous this year. Be sure you take one from the wagon outside when you go home. Take two, in fact." He winked at her.

Sabine Anker tapped his arm again. "Stop with your flirting, Gerard. She doesn't need attention from an old man like you," she said with a teasing tone.

"Miss Thom doesn't mind, Liebling." He winked at her.

Julia glanced across the room and saw James Hunter talking to Dr. Parker. The injured man's arm was still in its sling, and Hunter was being protective of it, keeping his body turned away from the crowd so that it didn't get jostled. Julia was surprised to see the clockmaker at the event. He seemed to avoid any such public gatherings.

She excused herself and walked over to talk to the two men.

"Mr. Hunter, you must not be able to eat anything with that broken wing of yours. Can I get you something?"

Both Hunter and Dr. Parker looked startled when she arrived, as though they were talking about something inappropriate. Julia wondered if they'd been talking about her, because they both slammed their mouths shut as soon as she got within earshot.

"I'm fine, Miss Thom," Hunter finally said.

The men looked at their shoes or over Julia's shoulder. She tried again, "Dr. Parker, did you know there's a pumpkin for you outside? The Ankers brought enough for everyone."

Parker looked at her absently and nodded, though she didn't think he'd heard what she'd said.

"Excuse me," he said and moved off, leaving Julia looking at the side of Hunter's face.

"I'd better go as well, Miss Thom," Hunter said. "On second thought, I would like to try to have a slice of some of the loaves that are available. That's something I can eat with one hand."

He moved away, still shielding his arm and Julia was left standing by herself wondering what she'd done to offend both men.

CHAPTER NINETEEN

Sunday afternoon's were Julia's favorite time of the week. They were a time of freedom, in stark contrast to how they'd been when she lived with her parents. At home in New Westminster, Sundays had always meant visits with Mrs. Thom's friends and other people she wanted to impress. Julia got dragged along from an early age and had learned to sit quietly in her Sunday dresses, sip tea, and find new ways to tune out the gossip. Her father was always excused from these visits, which infuriated Julia. If she had to be tortured thusly, she wanted him to share the burden. But he cleverly used the excuse that after church he needed to prepare for the cases coming in the next week, and retreated to his study. What he actually did there was drink port, smoke his pipe and nap in his big, leather wing-backed chair.

Sundays in Horse were gloriously different. After church, Julia used the time to go for long rides with Stanley, something she knew would come to a halt fairly soon, once the snow arrived. As soon as she could politely manage, she excused herself from the crowd at the school and made her way to the livery. Gerard Anker pressed a pumpkin into her hands as she left and, not wanting to waste more of the day taking it home, she took it with her to the stables.

When she and Stanley returned from an afternoon of exploring the surrounding hills, she found Walt and Merrick in their usual Sunday afternoon spot; sitting in front of the livery, sleeves rolled up, drinking Walt's homemade whisky from tin cups. The dogs were lying in the dirt and thumping their tails as Julia walked past.

When Stanley was groomed and bedded down with fresh straw and a scoop of oats in his bucket, Julia picked up a chair from just inside the barn doors and took it outside to join the men. Walt handed her a tin cup as she sat down. Her stomach was rumbling, and she was looking forward to a dinner of soup and fresh buns that Betty had given her, but she took the cup anyway, feeling reckless and invigorated after her ride.

She took a sip of the whisky and shivered as it went down.

"Where'd you get that hat?" Merrick asked her. He seemed more relaxed than Julia had seen him before.

"My father gave it to me. To keep the sun off my face when I ride."

"You know it's a man's hat, right?"

It was the black, wide-brimmed hat of the type a drover would wear. Julia liked it because the crown wasn't too high. She thought she looked dangerous in it, which pleased her. Also, because it was a man's hat, it fit her head, which was enormous. Her mother always complained that she could never find hats for church that fit Julia.

"Lemme see it." Merrick put his cup down on the ground beside his chair and held his hand out.

Julia looked at Walt. "Is he drunk?"

"I am not," Merrick answered, and leaned forward with his arm outstretched.

Walt nodded at her. "A little bit," he said quietly, smiling.

Merrick took Julia's hat from her hand and put it on his head, where it fit perfectly. He looked at her out from under the brim. "Do I look like you now? Do I look like a school-teacher?" He looked over at Walt, "What do you think? Could I be Miss Thom at school tomorrow?"

Walt squinted at him. "Say something scholarly."

Merrick's eyes turned back to Julia, "If you're going to do my job, I could do yours. We could swoop."

Julia smiled at him. "I think you mean swap."

"Swamp," Merrick muttered to himself.

Walt stood, set his tin mug on his chair and walked into the livery.

Merrick watched him go and then commented, "Nature calls, I expect."

With Walt gone, it was just the two of them. Julia tried to remember the last time she'd been alone with Merrick when they weren't arguing. She met his eyes and smiled at him, feeling a little self-conscious. He looked really good in her hat, she had to admit. The brim threw his eyes into shadow and made him look a little bit dangerous too. She liked this.

A thought crossed Merrick's mind. Julia saw it as clearly as if the shadow of a cloud had passed over his face. He looked away for a moment, and Julia imagined she could see him considering whether to share his thought with her. When he looked back at her, his blue-green eyes looked at her so directly she nearly had to look away.

"I did enjoy the dance the other night, you know." The whisky had clearly loosened his tongue. He stopped for a moment, having reached the cliff's edge, and then rushed on. "With you, I mean. The dance with you. Not just the dance in general." He made a swirling motion with his free hand.

This was completely unexpected. After she had hurt him unintentionally by trying to let him off the hook at the dance she assumed he thought negatively of the event. Around her, Julia felt the world become very still. Merrick's vulnerability surprised her, and she also noticed she felt a rush of pleasurable fear. He was waiting for her to respond. She felt a nearly crushing pressure not to hurt him again.

Their eyes were still meeting, and Julia was about to speak, when Walt appeared again from the livery entrance. "Who wants more grog?" he asked.

Merrick had been leaning forward, and now he sat up again and held his mug out toward Walt. "Just a bit."

Kicking herself, Julia held out her cup, just for something to do. Walt filled it and then for an instant turned away to set the jug down behind his chair. Merrick wasn't looking at her. He was staring at his boots. But quick as a snake strike she reached out and tapped him on his knee.

His head jerked up and he met her eyes.

"Me, too," she said quietly. And then again, "Me, too, Merrick."

The constable's mouth lifted just slightly at the corners and relief flooded through Julia's arms and torso.

Walt lowered himself into his seat and stretched his long legs out in front of him. "Are you going to join us at next week's poker game?" He looked at Julia and grinned. "I liked it that you ruffled Mayor Billy's feathers."

For the next few moments the three friends relived the game, though Julia declined to commit to joining the men on the following Thursday night.

After awhile, Julia felt Merrick watching her again. She turned and met his eyes as he asked, "Is this where you wanted to be?"

She tilted her head. "At the livery?"

"No. I mean here in the middle of nowhere. Is this what you pictured for yourself when you were a child? Being a schoolteacher, alone, in a town the size of my right boot? Is that what you wanted?"

Julia looked at Walt. "Why is he so philosophical all of a sudden?"

Walt shrugged. "Probably the grog."

She looked back to Merrick. "No. It isn't," she said, answering his question.

"Me, neither. I am the son of a farmer. Didja know that?"

"You've mentioned it."

"Well, I have. I mean, I am. I never in a million years thought I'd end up all the way across this country. In this beautiful place." He looked out across the rooftops of the stores across the street, into the hills that surrounded Horse.

Julia grinned at Walt. "I think you better cut him off."

Walt grinned back. "I already have."

"Now listen," Merrick continued. "I asked you a question. What did you imagine you'd be doing when you grew up?"

The afternoon light was fading and soon they'd have to go inside, out of the chill. There were some cotton wool clouds drifting lazily above them. Julia was pleased that they didn't look like the type that carried snow. She stretched her legs out and crossed her boots at the ankle. Merrick was watching her, waiting for an answer. The fact that he was a little tipsy amused her. She hadn't seen him this way before. He was usually a man in tight command of his emotions and his thoughts. She liked him more for the fact that he was being a little sloppy today. The fresh air and the whisky were having their effect on her as well; she decided to reward his pointed and inexplicable interest in her with the truth.

"I wanted to be a lawyer," she said and watched for his reaction.

He nodded slowly, bobbing his head up and down as though he didn't quite have control over the motion. She braced herself, waiting for him to laugh at the idea, as everyone did.

Finally he said, "You'd make a great lawyer."

Julia felt herself flush with pleasure and surprise. "Thank you."

"I mean it." He looked at Walt. "Wouldn't she? She'd be great at that."

Walt nodded. "Absolutely."

Merrick's eyes swam back to her. "You'd be fantastic as a lawyer. You're whip smart. You'd run circles around everyone. And you'd look great in a pin-striped suit."

Julia snorted, feeling shy and triumphant all at once.

"And," Merrick continued, "temperamentally you're perfectly suited for it. You can be real pushy."

Julia burst out laughing. A hearty belly laugh that flooded her with good feelings.

"I like this new, painfully honest you, Merrick," she said when she caught her breath. "I think we should keep you drunk all the time."

MONDAY MORNING, Julia felt groggy and had a hard time waking up. Her head hurt and her mouth felt like it was full of cotton wool. She had stayed with Walt and Merrick, chatting and sipping whisky for far too long the day before. She hadn't wanted the day to end after the two men had treated her crushed dream with such respect. Drinking whisky on an empty stomach hadn't done her any favors.

She got dressed and shuffled out to the kitchen. Forcing down her porridge, she wondered how she would manage her pupils in the state she was in. Perhaps another nature walk was in order.

She pulled on her hat and gloves and gathered together the books she wanted for that day's lessons. Every time she changed elevation - went from sitting to standing, or from standing to bending over - her head swam and she thought she might bring up the breakfast that had just gone down.

Boots buttoned, hat in place, stomach under control for the moment, she pulled open the front door of her house. As she went to step through it, something caught her eye. She turned, startled and looked at the open door, now beside her left shoulder. As quickly as she could, she stepped outside and vomited violently in her front garden.

There was a large hunting knife, with a blade at least eight inches long, stuck by its tip into her front door. Blood had dripped all over Julia's front step and down the length of the door because the knife blade was running through a small brown rabbit.

CHAPTER TWENTY

Merrick stood on Julia's front walk with his hands on his hips. He scowled at her front door.

Julia had left the rabbit and gone to find him. She was going to be late opening the school.

The blood on the doorstep was congealing; it looked like pudding from where Julia stood. The rabbit's head was hanging at an odd angle, its ears laying along its back. She felt very sad for the poor little beast and wanted to take him down right away, but knew she had to let Merrick do his job. At least the animal wasn't suffering. It had clearly been dead awhile.

Merrick didn't take his eyes off the front door. "And you're sure you didn't hear anything in the night?"

"Positive," Julia said. She didn't add that the whisky had pushed her into a deep sleep from which she was surprised to have risen. Her head still hurt. She glanced at the pile of vomit in her front garden, embarrassed to have Merrick see it. If he had noticed it, he hadn't mentioned it.

"Do you recognize the knife?"

Julia shook her head. "No."

"The men who threatened you at the dance had a knife."

It wasn't a question, but Julia answered anyway. "Yes."

"Does it look the same?"

Julia peered at her front door, looking at the blade and handle and trying not to see the rabbit. She tried comparing it to the fleeting impressions from the night of the dance. "I can't tell," she finally said, "This one looks bigger, but I can't say for sure."

Merrick nodded and then glanced at her. "Stay there." He walked closer to the front door, looking down, examining the ground for footprints, Julia guessed. He searched on both sides of the walkway. If the well-trod ground revealed anything to him, he didn't say.

When he was finished he went to the door and, grasping the knife in his left hand by its large wooden handle, pulled. The knife resisted for a moment and then came away, the rabbit with it. Merrick pointed the knife down at the ground and the animal slid off. He held it by its back legs and turned to look at Julia.

"Do you want some help cleaning up your doorstep?"

Julia was surprised by this offer. It seemed beyond the scope of Merrick's official duties.

She shook her head. "I need to get to school. I'll have to do it later."

He nodded once and then adjusted the knife in his hand. He seemed to be thinking about what he was going to say next. If he was embarrassed about his state the day before, he didn't show it. And unlike her, he didn't look green around the gills. "I want you to check in with me regularly. No going off riding without letting me know. No walking alone after dark. Are we clear?"

"Yes. Thank you, Merrick."

"I mean it, Julia." His expression was stern. "I don't know what the hell is going on, but someone clearly means to do you harm." He looked down at the knife and then back up to her. "Or at the very least, ensure you are afraid. I need you to keep me apprised of your movements until I figure out who did this." His gaze was steady, his eyes dark.

A drop of rain landed on Julia's face, and then another on her arm.

"I promise," she said.

Merrick nodded once. "C'mon. I'll walk you to school."

BETWEEN JULIA'S hangover and her shattered nerves, it was all she could do to hold it together for the day in the classroom. The children sensed her mood and, for once, didn't capitalize on it. They were quiet and subdued. The rain began in earnest as she opened the school doors. Her idea for a nature walk was dashed, so she had the students working on assignments quietly at their desks. She was not in a space where she felt competent enough to teach at the front of the room.

The children ate lunch inside. The rain came down in sheets, huge, fat drops one could see falling through the air, turning the schoolyard to a soupy swamp. By two o'clock the heavens took a break, and Julia made a spur of the moment decision to release the children early, yet again.

For the next several days Julia was never alone. The community made sure of that. That night Betty and Christopher had her over for dinner, though it was a strained and awkward affair since it turned out Christopher was still in Betty's bad books and Betty was hardly speaking to him. The appearance of peace at the Harvest Festival had been for show. On Tuesday, Betty and Julia received permission from Mr. Hunter to make soup at his home and tidy up. He was spending long days at his shop, trying to organize the mess that had been created when all the gears and clock workings had been swept onto the floor, as well as catch up on the repair jobs that were awaiting him.

The two women went to his shop after school, their arms weighed down with baskets of ingredients for soup.

Hunter looked at them over the counter, listening to the proposal to tidy up his house while they were there. He began to object but Betty pressed on, relentlessly. Julia suspected Betty was invested in this mission of mercy because she wanted desperately to be out of her own shop and away from her husband.

After a few moments of cajoling, Julia could almost see the resistance draining out of Hunter. He began to nod his head and then, to stop the incessant flow of Betty's argument, said, "Fine. Yes. Go ahead. The door is open." As an afterthought he added, "Thank you."

Julia and Betty let themselves into Hunter's home, lit the fire in the kitchen and then set to work, chopping vegetables and boiling water.

As they stood side-by-side at the table in Hunter's kitchen, each armed with a sharp knife, the rhythm of their chopping echoed around the room. Julia asked how things were going between Betty and Christopher.

Betty sighed, "Not all that well. I'm making him sleep in the guest room these days."

Julia sliced the top off of a carrot and began chopping it into chunks. "Does he have a plan for collecting any of the money he's owed?"

"He says he does. But I'm not sure he can follow through. Although, Albert Grimes was in the shop yesterday and wanted to use credit to buy his supplies. Christopher refused since he already owes us nearly twenty dollars."

"That's good, isn't it?"

Betty stepped over to the stove and tipped the cut vegetables on her cutting board into a large cast iron pot. "I suppose. But I was standing right there so he had to do it." Betty paused for a moment and then chuckled for the first time in a long time, "He looked like he might cry."

Julia looked over at her friend. "Oh, no."

"His face got all red and he stammered and spluttered. I just let him sweat it out. I pretended I was busy with the candles I was sorting."

"Betty Mitchell, I had no idea you were so cruel!"

Betty grimaced at Julia. "He has to learn, Julia. He has to figure out a way to not be the good guy all the time."

"That's not really who he is, though is it?"

Betty waved her knife around, her voice rising slightly, "He's going to have to figure out how to be that person. If he doesn't figure it out, we'll be living in your back garden."

When the soup was underway and Betty could manage on her own, Julia left the kitchen and began to dust and tidy around Hunter's small home.

The house, like his shop, smelled faintly of oil. She suspected this scent came home with Hunter from the clock repair shop, and that he didn't do any work here in the house. There wasn't a workspace laid out anywhere in the small house, at any rate. The smell was not unpleasant and it reminded Julia of her father and the times he had taken her to the shop where he got his pocket watches repaired.

She took a rag she'd brought and began dusting the living room. There were no photographs on display, though this was not entirely unusual. Photography was a new art and not everyone took the time, money or bother to go to a studio to have portraits made.

When she finished dusting she found Hunter's broom in a corner of the kitchen and began sweeping all the floors, creating piles of dust and dirt to pick up later. When she reached the bedroom she was especially thorough, noticing that the room didn't seem to have been swept out in some time. She worked the broom well into the corners and moved the tall dresser with some effort to sweep behind it. The bed was a narrow single, which Hunter had tucked into one corner. Julia reached the broom underneath it as best she could and then pulled the bed away from the wall to clean behind it as well. She stood the broom up against the door-frame and pulled at the metal frame of the bed. It shifted slightly but then stopped, caught on something. Julia crouched down and saw a small wooden box tucked all the way to the front of the bed, tight against the corner. The bed's leg couldn't move with the box in the way. Julia got on her hands and knees and reached under the bed, pulling the box back with her. It rattled slightly as she moved it and when it came fully out from under the bed, she saw it was an old apple crate filled with items wrapped in newspaper. Glancing at the bedroom door to make sure Betty wasn't watching her, and feeling slightly guilty, Julia delicately lifted the corner of a piece of yellowed newspaper to see what it held within. A patterned china plate with decorations of red roses around the perimeter and a blue ribbon flowing around them stared back at her. She closed the paper up again and pulled aside a different piece on the other side of the box. The same delicate china pattern emerged, this time on a tea cup.

Curiosity satisfied, Julia pulled the box across the room and then was able to move the bed. There was an old pair of boots under the bed as well. Julia moved these out into the middle of the room. She made a good job of cleaning under the bed and then put everything back where it had originally been.

The house began to smell very pleasantly of Betty's soup. When Julia finished sweeping her piles of dust outside, she found Betty rearranging preserve jars on the shelves in the kitchen.

"Hunter won't be able to find anything now," Julia teased her friend.

Betty glanced over her shoulder. "I can't help myself," she said, "it's the shopkeeper's curse."

CHAPTER TWENTY-ONE

The glove was bugging Julia. It had been sitting on her kitchen table for several days, but more than that, it had been preying on her mind. It didn't belong to James Hunter, that much was obvious. And whoever dropped it had not returned to claim it. This convinced Julia that it had to belong to whoever had assaulted the watchmaker. But how was she to find this person?

She spent Tuesday after school on her hands and knees scrubbing the floorboards in her kitchen. It was a thankless task that had to be done regularly to keep mice and bugs out of the kitchen. It was hard, unrewarding work and she hated it. (Although not as much as she'd hated cleaning the rabbit blood off her front step.) But the repetitive nature of the scrubbing, and the fact that her brain didn't need to be engaged in the task, allowed her mind to turn the problem over and examine it from several angles.

The glove was well-worn and constantly used. It was the glove of a working man, not a gentleman. Someone from a ranch, not from town. The mark across the palm was, she was sure, the groove of a reign, as she and Walt had discussed. It had to be. The trouble was that any man, anywhere, could own a glove like this. It had no distinguishing marks and nothing that made it different than a thousand other working gloves that must be in every house for five hundred miles around.

So what else did Julia know about it? She sloshed her scrub brush around in her bucket and thought. It was leather. It was an average size. Larger than Hunter's hands but pretty average for a normal man who wasn't as slight as Hunter. It was handmade, but that was not remarkable either. Nearly every article of clothing everyone wore was handmade. It was the right-hand glove. If the owner was right handed he'd be likely to hold his reins in his right hand.

So he worked with horses, that much Julia could be certain of. And the reign mark was so worn into the palm it had to mean the glove's owner was probably in the saddle more often than he was out of it.

Hunter still refused to speak about what had happened. A few times while Julia and Betty had been caring for him she had gently tried to approach the subject, but Hunter immediately closed down and clammed up. He still claimed he didn't remember any details from the attack, but Julia was convinced he was not telling the truth about that. Why he was hiding or protecting his attacker, she couldn't say. He was a reserved and private person, but this went beyond the need for privacy. He was actively discouraging Merrick and Julia from finding out who had attacked him. She was convinced this meant Hunter knew his attackers.

And yet, that didn't make sense to her. Hunter was not someone who was prone to being in conflict with others. He kept himself to himself. The very penchant he had for privacy was the thing that made it absurd that anyone had attacked him. He was the person in town least likely to cause upset or to offend. Julia just couldn't imagine Hunter upsetting anyone enough that they would try to resolve the problem by physically attacking him. It was like assaulting a straw man.

Whoever did this was a coward, Julia realized. Anyone with any courage would see that picking on Hunter was totally unfair; like shooting fish in a barrel.

The most logical explanation, given how little she knew, was that the attack was retaliation for Hunter helping her out on the night of the dance. Reluctantly, she brought to mind details about her attackers; their smell, their way of speaking, their size and height. She thought about their hands curling around her upper arms, their breath on her cheek and neck.

They had been drinking, and the memory of the smell of alcohol made Julia's throat close over. But she sat back on her heels, held the scrub brush away from her skirt, closed her eyes, and forced herself to focus.

Her fear and the pungent smell of fermented grain filled most of her senses. But there had to be more. In her mind's eye, she groped past the obvious and searched for the more subtle pieces of information that were there. She pictured the blackness of the night, the sound of the outhouse door closing behind her. She heard boots crunching on the dirt, not just her own boots, but others as well. The footsteps of the men behind her.

She shivered in the kitchen, but forced herself to keep her eyes closed and stay with the memory. One of the men, the one she thought of as First Man, had pressed the length of himself into her side once he had grabbed her arm, crowding her, using his size to intimidate her. He was wearing a long canvas jacket, she had sensed that it fell below his knees. They were both wearing hats, though she wasn't sure what kind. She had just a vague impression of this.

The scrubbing brush dripped water onto Julia's skirt. She had forgotten it. Were the men who attacked her the night of the dance and the person who attacked Hunter one and the same? There was no way to know. The two incidents could be totally unrelated. Hunter's beating could, in fact, be connected to his past. It might have nothing to do with Horse at all.

The glove's owner must work on a ranch. A drover or a ranch owner. She thought about the ranches around Horse and the operations they each performed. Not many ranches were yet able to hire employees. More often the owners did all the work themselves. Outfits such as Gerard Anker's Double A Ranch were the exception, not the rule. Julia suspected that Sabine Anker's money had something to do with that. Who else had a place that was doing well enough to hire help?

The word coward floated around Julia's mind, repeating itself, annoying her like a black fly. Why did it matter? she wondered. The character of the person who'd attacked Hunter was of less importance than who actually did it.

She opened her eyes and bent forward again, dipping her brush into the bucket to her right. Absently she ran it along the floor, no longer focused on her task. Something was gnawing at the edge of her consciousness but she couldn't bring it forward.

And then her father's face came unbidden to her mind's eye. His greying mustache and beard, his furrowed brow and eyes that watched sternly during his cases but until recently had almost always looked at his daughter with pride and love. She heard his voice in her head. *Bullies*, he had said to her more than once, *are, at their heart, cowards.*

She dropped the scrub brush into the bucket and stood up, pulling off her work apron. "Right you are, Father," she said to the kitchen and went to find her hat and riding gloves.

CHAPTER TWENTY-TWO

S he had to sneak out of town.

She wasn't sure where Merrick was that evening. But she was sure she needed to stay out of his sight. She took an indirect route from her house to the livery, avoiding the main street and the risk that Merrick would see her from his office.

While she groomed and saddled Stanley, she kept her ears attuned to Walt's rhythmic hammering from next door. It was almost like the drum in a band; the clang-clang as regular as clockwork.

When Stanley was saddled, she led him out of his stall. The animal automatically began to turn toward the front of the building but she guided him the other way, whispering to him. "This way today," and together they walked all the way down the center aisle and out into the paddocks at the back of the building.

Earl and Nelson were there, snacking on the hay Walt put out for them. They both looked up, eyes and ears interested, and watched as Julia and Stanley crossed to the far side of the enclosure. She opened the gate and led Stanley through and then closed it behind them. She glanced toward the back of the forge and listened. Walt was still tapping out his steady rhythm. She gathered Stanley's reins, put her left foot in the stirrup and floated lightly up into the saddle. When her skirt was adjusted, she clucked to Stanley and they trotted away, up the gentle slope that led out of town.

ALAN CECIL WORKED at the O'Brien Ranch, and it was him she was looking for. The word coward, with its insistent poking at her, and the memory of her father's belief about bullies, finally made her think of Alan Cecil.

She didn't know the man, really. All she knew of him was how she had seen him interact with his wife, Lily. And how Lily had reacted to him. That, it seemed, was more informative than his own behavior.

He was charming. He had exuded charm that night in the Finnegan's kitchen. Julia hadn't thought anything of it at the time, but when she pictured the scene, she remembered that Lily's demeanor had been odd. She was not a relaxed woman, by any stretch of the imagination. And what had bothered Julia at the time was that even when Lily's husband had been having a pleasant, jovial conversation with Julia, Lily hadn't relaxed.

It was subtle, and Julia didn't want to notice at first, but Alan Cecil seemed to have a strong hold over his wife. He had made that backhanded comment to her at the harvest festival, which seemed unkind. But it was the way he had been gripping his wife's arm in the kitchen at Finnegan's that stayed with Julia. It bothered her at the time but she had been distracted by Alan's subsequent charm and she hadn't let the moment register in the front of her consciousness. Now, though, it wouldn't leave her alone.

Alan Cecil worked with horses. This, combined with what Julia suspected was a slightly cruel nature covered up by a thin veneer of charm, was enough to make Julia want to talk to

Cecil. It was the slenderest of threads, but it was all she had. If she was totally honest with herself, she would realize that she was really on a wild goose chase. One that kept her from thinking about the poor rabbit on her front door and the danger to herself that this implied.

She had no information whatsoever that Hunter and Cecil even knew each other. Hunter was a refined, almost delicate person. Julia had never seen him on a horse. She wasn't sure he owned one. He spent his time, it seemed, within the town limits, working on his clocks and watches. Julia's limited experience of Alan Cecil was the polar opposite. Burly, ill-mannered, coarse, but with that vein of charm that appeared when needed. As far as Julia knew they had no friends in common other than Lily. Cecil lived and worked on the O'Brien ranch and stayed with Lily in her room at Finnegan's as often as his work would allow.

The hour-long ride gave her time to think, but rather than examining her own motives too closely, Julia focused on thinking about what she knew of Cecil. Which wasn't much. The couple was new to the area. They didn't have children, so that was not a point of contact for Julia. She knew they had lived in Kelowna before coming to Horse. Alan had worked as a stock manager for a ranch there, or so Millie Jones had said. It was unusual for Lily to work given that she was married. But the Cecils seemed to be making the best of an untraditional way of life. Alan lived in the bunkhouse with the other drovers, and that was no place for a woman. The arrangement they had for Lily to work and live at the Finnegan's made sense.

As Julia and Stanley followed the nearly invisible deer trail that led up and around the small hill they were climbing, she convinced herself that pursuing this line of inquiry was the right thing to do. Merrick might not agree. She patted Stanley's neck, reassuring herself with the feeling of his fur and muscles; distracting herself from this thought.

The O'Brien ranch came into sight. The chapel was the first building they passed as they came onto the land. The tiny building with its little steeple reminded Julia very much of her schoolhouse. Squat, longer than it was wide, with three tall windows down each side and a set of narrow steps leading up to the front door. The door was closed as they passed and Stanley barely gave it a glance. His focus was on the little cluster of outbuildings they came to next.

The barn was on her left, long and low, with two wide doors open on the side. She could see into the gloom inside as she approached.

Her heart was in her throat. It was as though suddenly her body and brain realized what she was doing. She'd come out here alone, searching for a man or men who she believed had already attacked two people; herself under cover of night, and Hunter in broad daylight.

Stanley felt her hesitation and stopped. She leaned forward, patting his neck, again seeking reassurance. His ears flicked around, noticing bird song and the movement of some tall grass near a fence post.

She thought for an instant about retreating, heading back into town, giving up her quest. Merrick was right; what she was doing was dangerous. She should heed the warning of the dead rabbit on her door. Whoever was behind the attacks was clearly deranged. What had possessed her to come out here by herself?

"Hello?"

Julia startled. A man came out of the barn, carrying a shovel in one hand and shielding his eyes from the sun with the other.

He was of medium build, though he looked thick and hard, like a large tree. His face was nondescript and his beard and mustache were almost entirely white, but the hair that poked out from under his peaked cap looked nearly black. His lips were pulled back slightly and Julia could see he was missing a canine tooth. His work shirt was buttoned all the way to his neck, but he wore no tie. His expression was questioning but his eyes looked kind. He was older than Julia by at least two decades but he didn't seem burdened by his age, as some men do.

"Hello," Julia replied, still debating about leaving without completing her mission. "I'm, uh, I'm..."

"You're Miss Thom from the school." The man completed for her. "Had you forgotten that?"

Julia could see he was teasing her; his eyes were alive with delight. She smiled down at him. "No, I, um. I know who I am. I'm afraid I don't know your name."

"Cobbs," he said, still holding his palm up to shield his eyes. "Spenser Cobbs, Miss. How can I help? Are you lost? Town's thataway." He gave a little jerk of his head back in the direction Julia had come.

Well, I've come all this way, Julia thought. "I'm looking for Alan Cecil," she said.

If Mr. Cobbs wondered why the schoolteacher was out on her own searching the ranch for a young drover, he didn't let that thought show on his face. He glanced up at the sky. "It's about supper time," he said. "The men will be eating in the cookhouse today, since they're working close by." He paused, thinking. "Why don't you leave your horse here and we'll walk over? I'll show you the way."

Julia tried swallowing but her throat wouldn't cooperate. So she threw her leg over Stanley's neck and hopped down to the ground instead.

Cobbs watched her quietly. When he turned to go back into the barn he said over his shoulder, "Not a fan of the side saddle, I see."

"No, sir."

"Good for you, young lady. Those things are a death trap."

CHAPTER TWENTY-THREE

The cookhouse was just that. A building about the size of the church Julia had just passed, but without any adornment. Julia imagined that there would be at least two large cook stoves inside, along with tables, and benches for the men to sit on when they ate. But today, in the cool but pleasant evening air, they were taking their meal *en plein*, as her drawing teacher Mr. Albert would have said. Seven men sat on wooden chairs with broken or missing backs a few feet away from a large river-stone fireplace. The wood crackled as Julia and Cobbs approached. A fat man in a stained white apron handed a drover with a tear in the knee of his pants a bowl filled with what Julia suspected was some sort of stew or chili.

The men's heads all swiveled in Julia's direction as she approached with Cobbs, but they didn't stop eating. They reminded Julia of a small herd of cows; eyes still, jaws moving.

"Want some supper?" Cobbs asked her, <u>sotto voce.</u>

She shook her head. "I ate before I came." Which was a lie, but she was anxious and didn't want to seem too familiar with the men.

Cobbs nodded once and then raised his voice. "Cecil. Miss Thom here would like to speak to you."

One of the men muttered something which Julia assumed was rude because the men on either side of him laughed, showing dirty teeth and partially chewed supper.

Alan Cecil was sitting flat on the ground, his legs stretched out in front of him, toes pointed toward the sky. His back was curled over his lap so he could spoon his supper to his mouth without dripping on his shirt. There was a large, torn chunk of bread at the edge of his bowl. He dipped it into the stew and then took a bite, watching Julia the whole time.

"What about?" he directed his question at Cobbs who didn't answer.

"Perhaps we could speak in private, Mr. Cecil?" Julia glanced around at the other men, who hadn't taken their collective gaze off her.

"Perhaps not," Cecil said, raising his voice doing an imitation of her. The other men chuckled.

They were sitting in a semi-circle, some on the ground and some on the old chairs. None of the men had stood up in her presence.

The charm that Cecil had exhibited in Finnegan's kitchen was entirely absent. His eyes had flicked to his companions when he'd imitated Julia, noticing their reaction and, Julia suspected, seeking approval. Here was a man, Julia reasoned, who was unsure of himself. In the presence of his wife, he had been confident and clearly was the more powerful of the two. Now, surrounded by other men, he seemed shrunken somehow. His sense of his own power was conditional; it depended upon who he was with. Julia made a note of this and wondered how Cecil would feel around another man such as James Hunter, one who was refined and not likely to provide a physical threat, as she was sure these drovers did. Would Hunter, who had some sort of relationship with Cecil's wife in the past, prove a threat to Cecil?

Just inside the cookhouse building, lying in an open doorway, Julia spotted a milking stool, lying on its side. She walked over the ten feet to it, picked it up, and carried it back to the group. She set it beside Cecil, gathered her skirt behind her and sat down.

The men had obviously hoped to intimidate her by making her feel unwelcome. When she sat down, the man to Cecil's left hesitated in mid-chew. She wondered how often a woman stood up to these men. She further wondered how often they encountered a woman who was not their mother, sister, wife or a woman they were meeting for the first and last time in a bawdy house.

As she did very often these days when she needed courage, Julia decided to pretend the group in front of her were seven schoolboys and that she was in charge of them. She looked around at them, letting her eyes linger on each face, committing them to memory and trying to see if her body reacted to the sight of any of them. If it remembered any of them from the night of the dance, though she consciously did not. Each face was lined and brown from the sun. All of the men were young, probably younger than her. They had thick, rough fingers with filthy nails and their clothes were dirty and patched. One fellow, directly opposite her, had his feet stretched out like Cecil did, and Julia saw he had a hole in the sole of one boot.

Each of them looked away from her when she met their gaze. Some lasted a few seconds longer than others, but they all broke their eyes from hers first and busied themselves with their meals.

She considered this a victory. Also, she noticed her body hadn't reacted to any of their faces. Both these things gave her courage.

"Mr. Cecil," she said, turning to the man on her left, and adopting her clearest and calmest but most no-nonsense voice, "was it you who attacked Mr. James Hunter in his shop the other day?"

This was obviously not the question Cecil had been

expecting. His spoon paused half-way to his mouth, his jaw partway open. She watched his eyes carefully. They registered curiosity and a lack of understanding, but Julia wasn't sure if they also held guilt.

He covered whatever he was thinking by finishing the spoon's journey to its target. "Wha?" he said around his mouthful of stew. "Who?"

This last question was for sure a lie. Julia could tell that right away that Cecil knew perfectly well who Hunter was. She could see it in his eyes before he glanced away, looking down at his bowl.

"James Hunter the sissy, you mean?" This was from a man across the circle. He had finished his supper and set the bowl beside the seat he was on. He was leaning forward, elbows on knees, rolling tobacco into a cigarette paper. He looked up at Julia with a confident expression. She glanced at the other men and saw most of them were watching him. This, then, was their de facto leader.

"What do you mean, 'sissy,' Mr....?" Julia let the end of the sentence ask the question for her.

"Roberts," he said, licking the edge of the paper. He sat up straight, owning the moment, and put the cigarette into his mouth. From his front pants' pocket he pulled a box of matches and lit one, inhaling the smoke from his cigarette and then tossing the match into the cook's fire. Roberts looked back at Julia. "He's the girliest man I've ever seen. That's what I mean by 'sissy.' If he tried to fuck a sheep I'm sure it would have its way with him first."

The other men laughed on cue, a little too loudly, proclaiming their allegiance to Roberts. When the noise quieted down, they looked back to Julia. *Your move*, their expressions said.

"I meant Mr. Hunter the watchmaker," Julia said, doing her best front of the room stare at Roberts. He picked a piece of tobacco off his tongue and flicked it away, shrugging.

She turned her gaze back to Cecil, and raised her eyebrows, "Well?"

Cecil scrunched up his nose and shook his head. "What're you asking me for?"

Julia answered his question with a question. "Is this yours?" She held out the glove. She had brought it with her in her saddlebag and transferred it to her coat pocket when Cobbs showed her to a stall where she could leave Stanley.

Cecil glanced down at it, and then away, shaking his head. He looked indifferent but she couldn't be sure if it was feigned or not.

"Where are your work gloves?" Julia asked, pushing Cecil.

He held his bowl in his left hand and reached around his back with his right, pulling a pair of gloves out of his waistband and showing them to her. He smirked at her while he did so, and then put them back.

"Has anyone else lost a glove?" Julia looked around the group, but the men just stared back at her, some chewing, some smoking.

She was getting nowhere. She met Cecil's eyes once more and he quickly looked away.

She stood up from the milking stool and tucked the glove back into her pocket. "Thank you, gentlemen," she said and began to walk away.

From behind her she heard Roberts' voice. "Don't leave yet. Each of us needs to have a turn."

Cobbs had hardly spoken since he and Julia had arrived at the cookhouse. He had fallen in beside her to walk her back to the barn.

He turned now and stared at Roberts. "Say that again."

The group was quiet. Roberts' and Cobbs' eyes were locked. For a few seconds Roberts kept a smug and self-satisfied grin on his face. Cobbs continued to stare at him and eventually Roberts' expression fell. He shifted in his seat slightly, and took a pull on his nearly finished cigarette. Cobbs waited, patiently, like the earth. Roberts moved again in his seat, uncomfortable now under the weight of Cobbs' gaze.

"What?" he finally said to Cobbs, his tone sullen.

Cobbs only jerked his head in Julia's direction.

It took a moment, but then Roberts finally spoke. "I apologize, Miss."

Julia nodded and then began walking again. Cobbs lingered for a moment and then fell into step with her.

CHAPTER TWENTY-FOUR

Julia and Stanley took a circuitous route back to town. It was a gorgeous autumn evening with clear skies and a not-unpleasant crispness in the air. Everywhere the land was alive with birds and she saw what she thought was a fox disappear into a burrow at one point. She let Stanley choose the pace. At times he galloped so that she had to nearly close her eyes against the wind. Then he would slow and catch his breath before taking off again. He was enjoying himself immensely, as was his mistress, so Julia was in no rush to return home. Only when the light began to fade in earnest did she decide that perhaps they should think about making their way back to town.

Cobbs had given her a leg-up when they returned to the barn. When she was settled in the saddle, her reins gathered, she leaned down to shake the man's hand.

"Thank you, Mr. Cobbs. I appreciate your help. And I thank you for defending me just now." She nodded back in the direction of the cookhouse.

Cobbs placed a hand on Stanley's neck and looked up at her. "You're most welcome, Miss. May I offer you a bit of advice?"

"Of course."

"I can see you're a very independent lass. There's not many women who would come out to a place like this on their own. My wife was a bit like you. Smart. And stubborn." He smiled at the memory and shook his head slightly. "But if I ever tried to tell her what to do, she'd do the opposite, just to spite me, I think."

"She sounds like a colorful woman," Julia said.

"Aye. She was. She's been gone six years now. I miss her something fierce." He paused for a moment, reflecting. When he looked up into Julia's face again, his eyes were a little shiny. "Here's what I'm askin' you. Please don't be so stubborn that you can't see when people are trying to help you and keep you safe. D'you understand me?"

Julia nodded brightly, "I do, Mr. Cobbs. Thank you." She straightened her spine a bit and was about to squeeze Stanley's sides and turn his head.

But Cobbs continued, not letting her brush him off so easily. "I mean it, Miss. You're bright and capable. I can see that. Please don't be reckless with yourself."

Julia looked down into his face again. Earnestness and concern were painted all over his expression. Julia found her voice caught in her throat.

Cobbs spoke again before she could. "Don't let your need to prove yourself put you in danger."

Was this man a wizard? How did he know her so well after such a short period of time, Julia wondered.

She leaned down again and placed her hand on Cobb's arm and looked directly into his eyes. "I promise," she said.

"Good girl." Cobbs patted Stanley's neck one last time and stepped back, smiling at her. "Straight home now."

SHE ARRIVED BACK at the livery filled with the joy of being alive and the pleasant exhaustion that comes with hours spent outside. Stanley was happy too, she could tell. He shook his head and jingled his bit as they rode down Main Street. He was prancing almost, and made her laugh when he bounced sideways like a kitten after a crow lifted up off a hitching rail in front of the millinery. She was still laughing at him and chatting to him about his good mood as they rode through the wide barn doors and she prepared to dismount.

A voice came out of the gloom at the back of the building toward her. "Where have you been?"

She hopped down to the ground and lifted Stanley's reins over his head. "Merrick?"

The man strode toward her. She had seen him angry before but the expression on his face now was something new. He looked taller than usual and was taking long, determined strides, swallowing up the distance between them. He stopped when he was three feet away from her. "I asked you a question."

If there was one way to put Julia Thom's back up it was to boss her around. Cobbs had assessed her exactly right in that department. Merrick should know this by now, but he was obviously struggling with his emotions. Julia pretended she didn't know what he meant. "I was out for a ride."

"Where?"

"Around," she said, glaring at him. She heard a noise in the back of the barn and assumed Walt was back there somewhere.

"You went to the O'Brien ranch."

It wasn't a question so Julia didn't answer. She looped Stanley's reins over her left arm and began loosening the saddle girth. Stanley blew out a breath and shook his head, ears and mane flapping.

Merrick came around Stanley's head and stood close to Julia's left shoulder. "Answer me."

She turned and looked directly up into his face. "You didn't ask a question."

He was very still and his lips were pulled together in a thin line. He held her gaze for several beats without saying anything. When he spoke it was with exaggerated quiet. "Were you at the O'Brien ranch?"

Julia gave a quick nod, "Among other places."

"What other places?"

"Oh, we were just out for a ride mostly. It's a beautiful evening." She patted Stanley's neck. "Now, if you'll let me pass I want to unsaddle this sweaty boy and get him groomed."

"You will do nothing of the sort until I say so." Merrick raised his voice and pushed his face closer to Julia's. She leaned back instinctively. "Do you mean to tell me that you went to the O'Brien ranch all by yourself? What were you doing there? Talking to Alan Cecil, I expect."

That he knew all the details of her mission only put Julia's back up further. She raised her voice, telling him to mind his own business. Merrick countered, telling her that the safety of the town's inhabitants was his business.

"Oy!" A loud voice broke into the argument. "Take this shit outside. You're bothering the animals." Walt appeared and reached past Merrick to take Stanley's reins from Julia. Together he and the horse walked down the aisle toward Stanley's stall. Walt looked over his shoulder. "I mean it. Go outside." He pointed toward the open door.

Julia whirled on one heel and marched out of the building, kicking up dust with every step. Merrick followed her, and by some silent but mutual agreement they stood in the front yard of the livery and faced off.

The three livery dogs watched the angry pair for a moment and then slinked away, ears pulled back with concern.

When the pair stopped and stood facing one another, Julia opened her mouth to speak but Merrick cut her off, waving a finger under her nose. "Do you even know how dangerous it is for you to do something like that? O'Brien has two ex-convicts working for him. And the rest of his crew are not much better, just smarter. They haven't been caught doing something illegal yet. Those men would cut you up and eat you for breakfast without a second thought."

"And yet, here I am in one piece." Julia held her arms out proclaiming her status as a living person who was not, in fact, anyone's breakfast.

"Only by God's good grace. What on earth did you expect to accomplish by going out there? Besides taking a chance on getting yourself killed. Or worse."

Julia started to speak but Merrick held one finger up and didn't let her interrupt. "Someone means you harm. For chrissake, do I have to remind you about the rabbit staked on your front door?"

He was concerned about her, Julia could see that on his face. It was lined with real worry, not just anger at a woman who was trying to do his job for him. But now he had angered her. She had been frightened by the men at the ranch, and it was only because Cobbs had been with her that she had left the property unscathed, though she was loathe to admit this to herself. She was also disappointed that the trip offered her very little, if any, new information. She wasn't any closer to figuring out who had beaten up Hunter than she'd been the day before. Admitting this to Merrick when he had pushed her so far into a corner was all but impossible for her, despite his genuine concern.

Forgetting what she had promised Cobbs, Julia said, "I'd do it again in a heartbeat," she flung the words at him, "especially since *you're* not doing anything about figuring out who beat Hunter up."

Her words stung Merrick. She saw that immediately. If she had been any less angry she would have felt guilty about it.

Merrick was still and silent, watching her, taking deep breaths. The pause lengthened and Julia was about to say something else when he finally spoke, his voice quiet. "Are you safe? Did any harm come to you out there?"

The abrupt change of direction threw Julia. "I'm fine," she said. "There was a nice fellow there named Cobbs. He made sure I was safe."

Merrick nodded once. "Cobbs is a good man." He thought for a moment. "All right then." He turned and walked away.

Julia watched him go and for a second, though she didn't know why, she had to fight back tears.

Stanley's jaw was crunching on something when she found him and Walt in his stall. Walt had removed the horse's tack and was brushing him in long, firm strokes with a dandy brush. Julia leaned against the stall door and watched them for a moment.

The big Irishman finally spoke. "He's concerned about you, you know."

"I know."

"You can be a bit reckless, there, Miss Schoolteacher. What would your Ma think of ya?"

"She wouldn't be surprised at all." Julia sighed.

"Always a troublemaker were ya?"

"According to her, yes."

"What about yer da?" Walt ran his brush along Stanley's back. The horse's skin quivered slightly.

"He never really involved himself in disciplining me. We were more intellectual partners. He left the raising to Mother."

"I'm not sure what much o' that means, since I'm just a stupid Mick, but I do know this. There's no sense torturing Constable Jack Merrick. He's a good man trying to do a tough job."

"I know."

"Do ya?" Walt came around Stanley's rump and set the

brush he'd been using on the top of the half-door. He took a pick out of his back pocket and, bending over beside the horse, lifted up one of his back legs and began cleaning out his hooves. "'Cause you're acting like you don't care about him or anyone else."

Julia was chastened and her eyes threatened to fill up with tears again. How was it that twice in one evening, two different concerned men felt the need to tell her off? Walt was such a quiet man; he kept his own counsel to an almost painful degree. So for him to be speaking to Julia this way meant he really had strong feelings about the subject. She turned to walk away. "I'll go apologize to him."

Walt stood up. "Leave him for now. Let him cool off. He's almost as stubborn as you are, so you need to give him a few hours to come down off his anger. He won't hear you otherwise."

Julia nodded, accepting the advice.

"So," Walt continued, "after all that fuss, did you find out anything more about Hunter or who beat him?"

"Not really, no. I get the sense that Cecil is hiding something, but it could just be that he's naturally cagey."

"Aye. Those men usually have something to hide. It just might not be the thing you think it is."

"Does O'Brien make a habit of hiring criminals?" Julia's eyes widened with the memory. "Some of those fellows looked like they were born without souls."

"O'Brien is as cheap a bastard as you'll ever find. He pays his men almost nothing so the only type of drover he attracts are the ones who are desperate and can't get work anywhere else. No self-respecting rancher will hire them."

"What's Cobbs' story? He seemed like a good apple among the bad."

Walt finished with Stanley's hooves and came and stood just inside the stall door, his back leaning against one wall of the stall. "Now he's a good guy. But that's just O'Brien's blind luck. Cobbs is Mrs. O'Brien's brother. He's been working on that ranch since day one. He doesn't agree with his brother-in-law's hiring practices, but there's nothing he can do about it. Thanks be to God that the O'Brien's never had any girls."

"Just boys?"

"No, sadly, no wee ones a'tall. They weren't blessed with children, but maybe that's for the best. I can't see those men of O'Brien's being a good influence on boys either."

"Mrs. O'Brien must be quite lonely out there."

Walt shrugged. The providence of women were a mystery to him.

He gathered up the brush and comb and opened the stall door. Julia backed away, giving him room. Together they walked toward the tack room at the back of the building. Earl poked his head out of his stall and Walt gave it a rub as he walked by.

Speaking the word 'lonely' had sparked something in Julia. She would have been embarrassed if she'd known how revealing her next question was. "How long ago did Merrick's wife pass away?"

"Oh, about a year-and-a-half now." Walt placed the brush and pick in a box on the tack room's work bench.

"Her name was Charlotte?"

"Aye. She was a good woman. Quiet. Kind. Refined." Walt leaned against the bench, remembering. "I'm not sure what she was doing with Merrick. She were half his size. And very delicate. She loved pretty things. What she saw in a great galumphing oaf like him, I'll never know." He chuckled softly.

Julia could see that Walt had cared for Charlotte. "How long did you know her?"

"Not long. She got sick a few months after I arrived. She got a cold and then that seemed to get better. But then it came back, worse the second time. Then it went away again. And then just a few weeks later she got the influenza. I think she was weakened by the two previous illnesses and she just didn't have the strength to fight off the next one." Walt crossed his arms across his chest. "Merrick stayed with her day and night, nursing her. Doc Parker was there every day, a course. But sometimes, these things..." he shrugged gently.

Julia wasn't sure what to say. She wasn't really sure what had caused her to broach this subject. The livery was quiet, just the occasional snort or fart from one of the horses breaking the silence.

"Well," she finally said, "I suppose I'll go home and feed myself."

"Good idea," Walt said. "I'm off to Finnegan's for a pint."

Together they walked to the front of the building. Julia said her goodbyes and walked away, out onto Main Street and left toward her little house. Walt watched her go. He was quiet for another minute, and then said to himself, "Charlotte was a lovely lass but she never got a rise out of him as you do. That's for sure."

CHAPTER TWENTY-FIVE

"What if Alan Cecil didn't do it?"

"Julia, are you back to that again? Good grief. You're a dog with a bone." Christopher Mitchell closed the Jones' gate behind him with a click and positioned himself between his wife and Julia for the walk home.

The Mitchells and Julia had been invited to Mayor Billy's house for supper on this Wednesday evening. An invitation from the Joneses was, according to the hosts, the most coveted in town. Their regular guests might see things differently.

For one thing, Millie Jones was, without question, the worst cook west of the Rocky Mountains. What she couldn't burn, she turned to mush. Her desserts were flavorless, but made up for that by having the consistency of sand. And the jams and jellies that she sent everyone home with were reputed to be used by local furniture makers as glue. The only thing that saved these evenings for everyone was that Mayor Jones poured his whisky liberally and often. Evenings at the Joneses' were the only time Betty Mitchell ever took a drink.

The Joneses lived in what was undoubtedly Horse's finest house. In addition to being the town's mayor, Billy Jones was the manager at the local bank. The bank had built him a two-story house on a sloped street a few blocks above town center. From its vantage point the Joneses could survey the entire town right down to the lake. Julia imagined that Millie appreciated this very much, as it was easier than just surveying the town down her nose.

The guests gathered in the parlor while Millie fussed with the last of the preparations for dinner. She had hired a cook three weeks previously, but he quit in a temper three nights before. "He couldn't take direction," Millie explained to everyone as she bustled off to the kitchen.

"More likely he couldn't stand constant interference and criticism," Christopher whispered to Julia and Betty under his breath. Julia hid her laugh behind her cordial glass. The tension between Betty and her husband seemed to have eased up a bit in the last couple of days, for which Julia was very grateful.

The Finnegans were there, Edgar already looking at his pocket watch, loathe to be away from the hotel and restaurant. Caroline, on the other hand, looked like she might move in. She was settled comfortably into one of Billy's wingback chairs and cooed appreciatively when he put a stool under her feet. This was the first time Julia had ever seen Caroline sitting down.

Roy Meddy and his wife, Esther, were there as well. When Julia and the Mitchells arrived, the Meddys were standing near the parlor's fireplace, chatting to an extremely tall and wiry man with a shock of red hair that rose off his head like an ocean wave. Meddy glanced toward the door to the room when Julia entered and then looked away again. But he did a double take when his brain processed who he was seeing. Julia gave him a little wave and noticed Mrs. Meddy watching this exchange with hooded eyes.

Music played in the hallway just outside the parlor door from a brand new disc cylinder box that Billy was very proud of. He was walking Edgar through its specifications and cutting edge technology; showing him the shiny silver-colored discs that somehow made the music. The parlor was a little too warm; Millie always overdid everything. Her meals were overcooked, her clothes were overly ostentatious and overly tight, her voice always seemed to be raised. So in the name of comfort she had laid a fire in the stove in the corner of the room, even though the night didn't really call for it.

This was Julia's first invitation to the Joneses, something Betty had warned her was coming. The parlor was impressive, with a glass chandelier hanging from the center of the ceiling, burning short, narrow candles. The receptacles that held the candles were light green and shaped like delicate flower petals.

"That's Venetian glass," Millie pointed out when she showed Julia around. "From Venice, *Italy*."

The wallpaper was flecked with something that sparkled in the light and all the furniture had matching flowered upholstery that, even to Julia's undomesticated eye, looked like it must have cost the earth. She had to suppress a child-like urge to wipe something sticky on it.

Conversation flowed and the guests were just beginning to relax when Millie burst into the room, red and sweaty of face.

"Dinner is served, everyone. If you will please follow me."

If Julia thought the parlor was fancy, the dining room put it to shame. The room was almost as wide as the house, and had a table that stretched from end to end, that could easily seat twenty. Millie had pulled out all her best china and silverware. As Julia sat down she noticed each silver piece had a crest with a stylized J for Jones. The last time she had seen such custom-made flatware was at her mother's home. Though Mrs. Thom used her set only at Christmas and Easter.

Julia was distracted all evening and it hadn't even registered with her until halfway through the meal that the gentleman with the buoyant red hair, who was now seated to her right, had been invited specifically as a potential match for her. His name was Theodore Cranna and he 'hailed' (as he put it) from a town on the Atlantic coast of Scotland that Julia immediately forgot the name of, so busy was she thinking about Hunter and her mystery. In addition to his thick red hair, Cranna had a red beard and a complexion that blushed easily and often.

He passed a china tureen to Julia which she guessed contained mashed potatoes, but couldn't be completely positive based on their appearance and smell.

"How do you enjoy being the local schoolteacher, Miss Thom?" Cranna asked.

"I love it," she said, scooping a sticky mass of black-flecked starch onto her plate. "Every day is different. The children are curious and engaged with their learning. And they teach me so much."

"Really?" Cranna asked, cutting a small piece of the grey meat on his plate. "What do you learn from them?" He sounded genuinely interested, so Julia answered him honestly.

"They don't make the same kind of assumptions we do," she said after a moment's thought. "They leave their minds open and very often are willing to engage a wider range of possibilities for an answer to a problem."

"I'm not sure I would give children that much credit."

"They might surprise you, Mr. Cranna."

Millie Jones happened to catch the tail end of this conversation and used it as a means to tell the latest story about her 'genius' grandson who was destined to be both a famous scientist and one of the future prime ministers of their new country.

Julia listened with half an ear. Most of her attention was on replaying the afternoon she'd had at O'Brien's ranch and her exchange with Alan Cecil. Was it a flash of recognition in Cecil's eyes she had seen when she showed him the glove? Or was it something else?

She felt Betty poke her in the ribs.

"What?" she turned to her friend.

"Mrs. Jones was just asking you a question."

Julia turned to her host. "I'm sorry, Mrs. Jones. I didn't hear you."

"I was just asking," Millie sniffed, registering displeasure at not being the very center of everyone's attention, "if you will take the same liberal approach with your own children as you do with the ones in the school?"

Julia was slightly taken aback by the question. Because she hadn't been paying attention she wasn't sure of its context. And also, it seemed impertinent. Certainly not dinner table conversation with mixed company. Millie Jones set Julia's teeth on edge at the best of times, and this was definitely not the best of times. She lobbed the question back at her host. "What children of my own?"

Millie tried smiling but it looked more like a sneer. "Your future children, of course, Miss Thom. I'm aware you're not a mother now." She tittered at Cranna who was very obviously the beneficiary of this topic of conversation.

Julia was rapidly discovering that in a small town, other people's business was a primary source of occupation and entertainment. This did not sit well with her and yet she hadn't figured out yet how to draw a boundary around what she was unwilling to offer for public consumption without being rude. She also knew, though, that Millie didn't take hints. You had to bang her over the head with a point if you wanted her to get it.

"I'm not sure there are children in my future, Mrs. Jones. Other than the ones I teach."

Millie tapped the corners of her mouth with her napkin. "Don't be hard on yourself, Miss Thom," she said. "You'll find a husband one day. Your penchant for riding astride a horse won't offend every man. I'm sure there are some men who might find that kind of..." she searched for a word, "unorthodox and inappropriate behavior charming in some way. Wouldn't you say, Mr. Cranna?"

Cranna was obviously stunned to be drawn into this sudden sparring match. He spluttered a bit, swiveling his head back and forth, caught between his hostess on his right and his intended match on his left.

Julia rescued him, "Luckily, men of that sort - the kind who welcome independent thinking and other nonsense - are few and far between, Mrs. Jones. I needn't worry because what I meant was that I'm not sure I want to have children. If I married and had children I'd have to stop teaching, and that doesn't appeal to me."

Millie made a noise that sounded like 'Pwwaa' and her startled eyes darted around the table. "Surely you don't mean that! Who would voluntarily remain a spinster?" She laughed at the absurdity of it all.

"Not everyone can be as lucky as Betty and Christopher and find true love," Julia said as she touched her friend's arm. "Besides what's wrong with wanting a career?"

"Nothing in the least," Millie countered, "as long as it's temporary and a woman quickly finds her place in her home and with her children." She looked at Cranna with an expression that suggested Julia had just bought a one-way ticket to the home for the mentally infirm. "Besides, where does 'love' fit in with all this? A marriage is a partnership, a business if you like. Mr. and Mrs. Mitchell know that full well. They literally run a business together. And I'm sure they'll be producing children very soon, as well."

Millie smiled benevolently at Betty, unaware she'd just wounded her guest, who was unable to have children, and very sad about it.

Julia reached for Betty's hand under the table and squeezed it.

. . .

Much to Julia's relief, Millie turned her attention elsewhere for the rest of the meal. She was not so lucky with Mr. Cranna. He chatted to her about Scotland and his travels that took him through the Panama Canal and up to San Francisco. When, for the third time, Betty had to kick her gently under the table because she'd drifted off and had missed a cue from Cranna to ask a question, Julia reluctantly dragged her mind away from the puzzle of Mr. Hunter.

"Tell me about San Francisco," she said, taking pity on the tall, awkward man.

He looked so genuinely pleased to have Julia's attention that she felt guilty about the way she'd treated him thus far.

"The architecture is something to see, Miss Thom. I stayed for one night at the Palace Hotel, and oh my," his eyes widened at the memory, "you can see the building for miles around. It's taller than you can even imagine. And inside, right in the middle of the building, at the very top, there's a huge skylight that floods the building with light. It is so perfectly impressive. Each hotel room has its own bathroom." He stopped and waited for Julia's reaction.

"Amazing," she said, mustering the polite interest her mother had instilled in her, "you were so lucky to have spent a night there."

"Well," Cranna almost wriggled in his seat with pleasure, "one night was all I could afford, but I couldn't leave town without at least experiencing it."

By the time dessert and coffee were served, Julia knew as much about San Francisco as if she'd been there herself. To her dismay, Millie orchestrated things so that Cranna was able to position himself beside Julia in the parlor after the meal. He continued their conversation by detailing for her the horrors of oceanic travel and the seasickness he never got over until he was on dry land again. Julia felt her nearly-inedible supper roiling in her stomach at his descriptions and eventually had to ask him to stop, fearing she might throw up on

Millie Jones' Persian rug. ("From <u>Persia</u>," as Millie had pointed out.)

"I'm so sorry, Miss Thom. I've been prattling on. You must find me boring in the extreme."

"Oh no, Mr. Cranna," Julia lied. "The picture you paint of your voyage is fascinating." She hoped she didn't sound too insincere.

"Tell me," Cranna said, "what do you enjoy most about teaching?"

Julia was amused that Cranna had enough self-awareness to notice that his conversation partner was in need of some attention. "It's challenging. Especially teaching such varied ages. But I love it."

"How old are they?" He seemed genuinely interested.

"The youngest is seven, and the eldest is fourteen."

"They must adore you."

"Not when I make them do math sums."

Cranna continued asking her questions about her work and her life in Horse. He tried to hide his shock when he learned that she lived alone.

"I thought you lived with the Mitchells."

"No. They're good friends but I live on my own. In a little house the school board provides for me."

"Really?" He thought about this for a moment. "I can't see it."

"What do you mean?"

"I mean I can't imagine it. A woman living on her own."

"You don't have to imagine it, Mr. Cranna. It's happening."

Roy Meddy glowered at Julia throughout the meal from his seat across the table. He said very little to his wife who was on one side of him, or to Mayor Billy who was on the other. Esther Meddy and the mayor seemed to be passionately debating something. Millie had to shush them several times when the debate became heated. Julia hadn't caught the subject, but when the mayor and Mrs. Meddy continued their politely veiled argument in the parlor after dinner, she saw that whatever it was it meant a tremendous amount to both of them.

Cranna excused himself momentarily from Julia's side, and like a shot Roy Meddy was at her elbow.

"Did you figure out how that little sissy Hunter managed to cheat at the poker game?" he stage whispered.

Julia took her time answering, eyeing the baker coolly. "I'm not sure I understand, Mr. Meddy. That's not my concern. What I'm trying to find out is who beat Mr. Hunter."

"I'll tell you this." Meddy lowered his voice even further. "When you find out who that little turd really is, then you'll have the answer to who put the boots to him."

"What on earth do you mean, Mr. Meddy?"

"Just that. And I'll also tell you this…" However, Meddy was interrupted by his wife, who pulled herself away from the mayor and came across the parlor floor to her husband's side.

"We must go, Roy," she said, barely glancing at Julia. "Morning comes far too early."

When they left, Julia was still puzzling over what Meddy meant about finding out who Hunter was.

"THAT ODIOUS WOMAN makes my head ache." Betty struggled pulling on her gloves and finally gave up and shoved them in her pocket, taking her husband's arm. "And that food! I'm starving, Christopher. I hope we have some of that soup left because I'll need it when we get home. I could hardly choke down whatever that meal was supposed to be."

"I think it was roast pork with potatoes and greens."

"More like roast arse." Betty was never as rude as when she'd just spent time with Millie Jones.

Julia chuckled. "How does she manage to insult everyone at the table in the span of two minutes?"

"Cranna emerged unscathed," Christopher pointed out.

"I don't know," Julia countered, "the implication was that any man who was attracted to me had to be touched in the head. I do think the intention, however, was to get Cranna to like me. Implying that he was too stupid to run the other way."

"Good luck with that," Betty said.

"Hey!"

"I didn't mean you're not immeasurably attractive, my darling." Betty reached across her husband and patted her friend's arm. "And thank you, by the way, for pulling the spotlight off me after that 'when you and Christopher have children' comment."

"My pleasure."

"What I meant was that Cranna didn't stand a chance. You're so preoccupied with this issue with James Hunter that you hardly heard a word anyone said."

"I made an effort to listen to Mr. Cranna and his tales of travel. You'd think he was the only person to ever cross the Atlantic," Julia huffed.

"He seems a decent sort," Christopher said.

Julia relented, lowering her voice, "Oh, he was fine. I'm just grumpy because I'm hungry and preoccupied." That was when she asked, "What if Alan Cecil didn't do it?" She followed with, "Also, Roy Meddy said the strangest thing tonight. He made a comment about 'figuring out who Hunter really is'."

"What do you think he meant?" Betty asked.

"I have no idea."

Christopher was holding a lantern and guiding their way down the dark street.

"He still denies hurting Hunter. I'm not entirely sure I believe him though. What's your assessment of him, Betty?"

Betty thought for a few moments and then said, "He is an angry man, that's for sure. I've not yet had an encounter with him when he didn't seem like he was at the boiling point. Although I might act that way too if I was married to his wife."

"But do you think he could be physically violent?" Julia asked.

"There's no way to know really, is there? If you push almost anyone far enough, they'll resort to violence. Especially if they're trying to defend themselves."

"Whoever attacked Hunter wasn't acting defensively. At least, that's the way it looks to me."

Both women were quiet, thinking some more.

"What do you think, Christopher?" Julia asked.

Christopher glanced down at Julia. He seemed slightly startled to be included in the conversation. "Me? Oh, goodness. I have no idea."

Julia tried to jostle an opinion out of him, "Humor me, Christopher. Do you think Roy Meddy could be violent?"

"Well, now," he waffled a bit, "I don't like to think anyone could beat someone else up."

"But it happened. Do you think Meddy has it in him to attack someone like Hunter?"

"I don't think so. I can't see him doing that."

"But do you think it's possible?" Julia continued to press him.

"Well, I…you see, I think..." Christopher burbled a bit without saying anything.

Betty spoke up, "You won't be able to get him to commit, Julia. My husband can't think ill of anyone."

Julia detected a note of frost in Betty's voice. She suspected the couple had not completely resolved their argument about the store's financial position.

The trio turned at a corner and stepped up onto the sidewalk that ran in front of the shops in the Mitchell's General Store's block.

When they reached the store's front door, Betty turned to Julia. "Are you coming in for some soup?"

"Yes, please. I'm ravenous. How did Mayor Jones get so fat on that woman's food?"

"Love is blind," Christopher said and opened the general store's door for them. "And also without taste buds, apparently."

"JULIA, THIS MAKES ME VERY NERVOUS."

"Try to stay calm, Betty. We'll be out of here in two minutes."

"Why are we even doing this?" Betty glanced around her nervously.

"That thing Roy Meddy said last night won't leave me alone. I need to check something."

"What if he catches us?"

"Dr. Parker? We'll just say we were waiting for him. You'll tell him Christopher has a cough you're worried about."

"But he doesn't."

"He's cured. It's a miracle."

Julia stood at Dr. Parker's filing cabinet, swiftly flipping through the patient files in the top drawer. Each name was written on the edge of the file in Dr. Parker's small, precise printing. She had to squint to see many of the names but recognized almost every one.

Betty was standing in the doorway that led from the front hall of the house to the office, watching the street through a front window, her face screwed up with anxiety. "Oh, this is terrible," she muttered to herself, "terrible. How did I let you talk me into this?"

"Because you're a good friend and you like a little adventure as much as the next gal," Julia said. "Admit it."

Betty was silent, not willing to admit her friend was right. She might be morally compromised by helping Julia break into the doctor's office, but part of her was thrilled with the danger. This was a part of her she didn't like to show to anyone, nor admit to.

"Here he comes. He's just leaving Finnegan's."

Julia closed the drawer and opened the one below it.

"What are you doing?" Betty glanced at her friend. "Didn't you hear me? He's coming."

"We've got a few minutes. Calm down."

"Gracious, Julia, you're giving me a heart attack."

"Well then, we're in the right place."

The clock in Parker's living room ticked loudly, no doubt grating Betty Mitchell's nerves. "He's crossing the street now, by our store. Oh! He's stopped to talk to Pastor Thoreson."

"I'm done anyway. Let's go." Julia picked up her small beaded handbag off Parker's desk and strode toward the door, her expression preoccupied.

Betty fairly scurried down the hallway, launching herself at the front door's knob. "Did you find what you were looking for?"

"No."

"Oh," Betty's face fell. "That's too bad."

"Actually, it's the absence of the file I was looking for that tells me something." She followed Betty through the open door and closed it swiftly behind her.

CHAPTER TWENTY-SIX

Julia woke to the sound of shouting. Her head jerked off her pillow, and she sat in the dark, confused for several seconds, not sure where she was. She had been dreaming of home, of her parents. Her mind slowly caught up and she remembered that she was in her new bedroom in Horse. She could still smell the scent of her father's tobacco.

The shouting was outside.

She got up, wrapped the blanket from her bed around her shoulders, and went to the front room. Pulling the curtain aside, she looked out and saw two men running past on the street, lanterns in their hands. Something was wrong.

Julia got dressed as quickly as she could, pulling on an old cotton dress she used when she was cleaning, forgoing her corset and covering herself up with her thick wool coat. She pulled on her riding boots, which were close at hand, and left her hair hanging loosely down her back.

Closing her front door behind her, she ran out onto the street. As soon as she was halfway down her front walk, she could smell it.

Fire.

. . .

To a small town in an outback place there is nothing as terrifying as fire. The weather could be dealt with in many ways; it was possible to hunker down in snowstorms and slog through the muddy streets during the rains. The heat of the summer could be managed with shade and liquids. Horse was fortunate to be situated right beside a lake, which provided transportation, as well as drinking and washing water.

But fire was the one element that struck terror into every citizen's heart. It had the potential to sweep through a place, turning it to ash before almost anything could be done. It was like a beast that could not be fought back, ravenous and raging. Just four years earlier, many lives had been lost and countless buildings destroyed in Vancouver, when city workers lost control of a brush fire.

Julia ran toward the orange glow that lit up the night. The smell of burning wood filled her nostrils. As she got closer she could hear the wood crackling, like a giant camp fire. She ran to the end of her street and turned left, huddled in her coat. She could hear shouting over the noise of the burn; men's voices, frantic and loud.

It was James Hunter's house, she realized as she got close. The roof was ablaze and fire and smoke were pouring out of the front windows. A chain of men was using buckets and anything else handy to pull water from the lake and douse the flames. Julia immediately saw they wouldn't be able to save the house. Their objective now would be to prevent the fire from spreading. On one side of Hunter's home was an empty lot, which was a saving grace. On the other was the Carson family home.

Mrs. Carson and her two small boys were standing in their front yard, watching in horror.

Julia saw Merrick, Walt, Christopher Mitchell and Pastor Thoreson all in the bucket chain, faces fierce with concentration.

A voice came from behind her. "Where's Mr. Hunter?" It was Betty.

Julia turned and wrapped one of her arms around her friend. "Is he in the chain?"

They both looked down the line but couldn't see the home owner.

"He's not inside, is he?" Betty voiced Julia's thought.

The two women looked around at the crowd of women that was gathered. Every available man was pitching in.

Julia broke away from Betty and approached Mrs. Carson, raising her voice over the crackling of the fire. "Have you seen Mr. Hunter?"

The woman shook her head and pulled one of her boys closer to her.

Frantic now, Julia and Betty walked down the chain of water-bearers, staring into every face. When they reached the lake, they turned to one another, bleakness in their eyes.

"Come on." Julia grabbed Betty's hand and they ran back to near the top of the chain. Merrick and Walt were beside one another shifting buckets and pots, anything that would hold water, up the line toward the house.

"Have you seen Hunter?" Julia continued to hold Betty's hand.

Merrick shook his head and grabbed a bucket with a rope handle being passed to him. "No," he said. "Have you?"

"No."

The crackling of the fire got louder. The heat coming off it reached all the way back to where Julia and Betty stood. There was a crash from the house, and a plume of sparks rose up in the dark sky, disappearing almost as soon as Julia turned her head at the noise.

"Get back, will you?" Merrick asked. He was curt with them, but then added, "Please."

Julia and Betty curled into one another and moved away

from the chain, Julia's eyes fruitlessly scanning the orange dark all around them.

It was then that she spotted Hunter. He was standing two houses away, leaning against a fence, a hopeless expression on his face. He was wearing a long nightshirt that almost reached his ankles, and nothing else. His feet were bare.

Julia squeezed Betty's hand and pointed. They both began to run to where Hunter stood. Julia's gaze was caught momentarily when the bright orange light from the fire showed Hunter in silhouette in his nightshirt. She unbuttoned her coat as she ran and pulled her arms out of the sleeves. When she reached Hunter she threw the coat around him, pulling it tight.

"Mr. Hunter, you should come with us."

The man turned to Julia but his eyes were glassy. She wasn't sure he recognized her.

"James? It's Betty Mitchell and Julia Thom. We're going to take you away from this. Come on. There's no need to watch."

Together Betty and Julia slowly turned Hunter and began to walk with him, their backs to the blaze. Hunter crept along, his bare feet seemingly oblivious to the cold.

CHAPTER TWENTY-SEVEN

Julia's house was closest so she and Betty guided Hunter there. They settled Hunter on the settee, and Julia ran to grab a blanket off her bed. Hunter kept the coat wrapped around his shoulders, and though it was a comfortable temperature in the house, he shivered.

"Betty could you stoke the fire, please?"

Betty nodded and got a little blaze going in the pot-bellied parlor stove. Julia encouraged Hunter to ease back on the couch. She put a towel down for his feet, which were icy to the touch, and wrapped the ends of the towel around them.

When the fire was going, Julia got the kettle from the kitchen and brought it out to the parlor stove. She set it down on top and went to retrieve cups and the teapot from the kitchen.

Betty and Julia fussed over Hunter and the tea, the activity bringing comfort. When they finally settled, each into a chair, Hunter spoke for the first time.

"Do you think anyone else saw?" He looked at Julia.

"I don't know," she replied honestly, "It's possible."

Betty looked back and forth from Hunter to Julia. "Saw what?" she asked.

Hunter was quiet, staring into the middle distance without seeing.

Julia finally spoke up. "Do you want to tell her, Mr. Hunter?"

The man ran his tongue around his lips, still not looking at either of the women. Julia and Betty waited, both ignoring their tea.

Finally Hunter looked over at Julia. "How long have you known?"

"I had an inkling yesterday." She looked at Betty. "After our impromptu visit to Dr. Parker's."

Betty furrowed her brow, more confused than ever.

Hunter nodded, thinking. Then he looked over at Betty Mitchell and stood up. The blanket around his shoulders fell away. He took hold of Julia's coat, where it lay across his shoulders and pulled that off as well.

Betty turned her face away from the figure that now was housed in just a thin nightshirt.

Hunter's voice changed slightly, "Look, Mrs. Mitchell." Hunter pulled the nightshirt away from his sides so that it clung to his body across the front.

"Mr. Hunter," Betty said, looking away from him and wild-eyed at Julia, "please cover yourself."

Hunter sighed and continued holding his night shirt tight against his chest. "Please."

Betty's head snapped up at the change in tenor of Hunter's voice. She looked over finally and saw what Hunter was showing her. Where a man's smooth chest should be, the points of two small breasts could clearly be seen through the thin cotton night shirt.

"You might as well call me Evelyn," she said.

"HAVE SOME TEA." Julia motioned for Hunter/Evelyn to sit down. "And perhaps you'd like to unburden yourself to us."

Evelyn left the coat where it lay on the couch but pulled the blanket around herself and sat down. She took a sip of tea and then left the cup in its saucer while she told her story.

"I never felt at home in my body. It's really that simple. I never felt like 'me'. For the longest time I assumed everyone felt that way. But also," she stopped, looking down at her hands, "I knew something was wrong."

She had grown up the daughter of a watchmaker in what was then called Granville, now Vancouver. She had three brothers and a sister. It was the sister she finally confided in during a moment of vulnerability before her sister's wedding.

"It was the night before the wedding and we were excited and nervous, of course. It was to be our last night sleeping in our room at home. After the wedding she and her husband were moving to Victoria. I shared how I felt with her. I asked her if she felt at home in her body. She said yes and looked at me like I was crazy."

Julia could see the pain in Evelyn's face.

"I pressed on. I had to know how she felt. I had to find out before she was gone what her experience was like. She was horrified at my questions. She kept asking me to stop. But I couldn't once I'd started. Seventeen years of wondering what was wrong with me and waiting to feel...." She thought for a moment. "At peace."

But her sister hadn't been able to grasp what Evelyn was telling her. They argued and then Jane ended up sleeping in the living room for the rest of the night, uncomfortable with the conversation.

"She didn't look at me all the next day," Evelyn said. "And she left on her honeymoon without saying goodbye."

A few tears leaked out of Evelyn's eyes. Julia went to her bedroom and found a clean handkerchief and brought it back to the living room. She handed it to her guest. Evelyn took a huge breath and then let it out.

"So I left. I had some money saved up from working in my father's shop - he's a watchmaker, too. I bought a suit in secret. I told the shopkeeper it was for my husband." A rueful laugh. "And I made my way up here. Dressed as a man."

"But how... I don't understand. How did no one know?" Betty was leaning forward in her chair, fascinated and also horrified, though Julia could see she was trying to hide that part of her feelings.

Evelyn gave Betty a small, pursed smile. "Did you know?"

"I can't... I don't..." Betty sat up a little straighter, her hands clasped in her lap. She looked away for a moment, thinking and then looked back at Evelyn. "No. I didn't. How is that possible? It's so obvious now. Your smooth skin. Your small frame..." she trailed off.

"I've thought about this quite a bit, of course," Evelyn explained. "And I think the one conclusion I've reached is that people very often accept what we present to them. If you say you're a man, then people don't think about it too much."

Julia had been listening quietly through all this and reflected that this was certainly true for her. She had even been physically close to Evelyn when she and Merrick had helped him/her to Dr. Parker's office after the beating, and still she hadn't realized she was touching a woman. Her brain had been programmed to experience Evelyn as a man.

"Although," Evelyn continued, "sometimes people do catch on. I had a few very scary encounters in Vancouver before I moved up here." She looked over at Julia. "That's why I carry that little pistol with me. I've never fired it before that night at the dance. But it did come in handy a couple of times in the city. Waving it around would encourage those who were bothering me to leave me alone."

Betty's brow furrowed. "Are you more at peace living as a man?"

Evelyn nodded but it was a tiny gesture. "Yes. In many ways. It's odd because when I was living as a woman, a girl, I always felt like I was hiding something. Like I had a secret. Now that I'm..." she made a little motion with her hands, searching for a word, "*presenting* myself as a man, that feeling of secrecy has gone away. But it's been replaced by another kind of secrecy. Now I really *do* have something to hide. If people found out..." She let the end of the sentence linger.

Julia finally spoke. "I think someone has."

Evelyn nodded again. "I agree. Someone knows. That's why the beating. And the fire."

While they had been talking, the reason for their gathering faded into the background. At the mention of the fire, all three women were gripped once again by anxiety about what might be going on outside.

More as a way to keep their mind off this than a means to pry, Julia said, "Tell us about Lily Cecil."

"Ah yes. Lily. Well. She knows for sure." Evelyn settled back into the settee a bit, relaxing now that she had nothing to hide. "We went to school together."

"Small world," Julia said.

"Indeed. I specifically moved to Horse because it's far from anywhere and I thought I could live here in anonymity, hopefully for many years. But wouldn't you know it? I've only been here nine months and who do I bump into but a school chum, Lily Crewes. That's her maiden name."

"Did she recognize you right away?" Betty sipped her tea absently.

"On some level I think she did. She came into the shop one day looking for a second-hand watch for her husband's birthday. I knew instantly who she was, of course, but I kept quiet and hoped she wouldn't place me." Evelyn looked through the louvered door of the stove, watching the flames, remembering. "I could see it was confusing for her. She was being presented with a man's voice and body and attitude, but behind that I'm assuming she could see and remember me."

Betty anticipated Julia's question. "Did she say anything?"

"Not then. But she was distracted and puzzled, I could tell. She left the shop and I was left wondering what to do. I began considering moving to a larger center. Maybe Kelowna or maybe farther east."

"But she confronted you later. At your home after you'd been beaten." Julia filled in the blank.

"Yes." Evelyn looked at her. "You heard us, did you?"

"I didn't hear anything, but I saw the little confrontation you two were having. I thought maybe it was a lovers' spat. I wondered later if Alan Cecil had noticed anything between you and his wife."

"Yes, poor Alan." Evelyn smiled ironically. "I think he's jealous. But I begged Lily not to tell him. And poor Lily. She's been caught in the middle. I hope to disappear soon and put her out of her misery. That is, if I can." Evelyn glanced at Julia's front windows where the sky was just beginning to lighten. "My clothes have probably all burned up."

Julia wouldn't let her change the subject. "Do you think it was Alan Cecil who beat you up?"

Evelyn turned back to her host. "I honestly don't know. I was telling you and Constable Merrick the truth when I said I don't remember anything from that day. It's all a blank, going back to the previous evening. The last thing I remember is tidying up after supper. That's it."

"I went out the O'Brien ranch the other day to talk to him." At this Betty raised her eyebrows, but Julia pressed on. "He's not the smartest person alive, and I wonder if he just let his fists do the talking for him."

"It's possible." Evelyn pulled the blanket a little tighter around her shoulders.

"You seem like you're not convinced," Julia said.

Evelyn looked steadily at Julia. "I'm sure it's possible. It's just that Alan strikes me as a coward. A follower, not a leader. Someone who would abuse a woman, for sure. I don't think he treats Lily very well. But I'm not sure he has the backbone to attack another man."

This assessment agreed with what Julia observed in Cecil at the ranch.

Betty spoke for the first time in several minutes. "You must have fresh insights into the workings of the male mind."

Evelyn surprised them and shook her head. "Not fresh insights, no. I've always felt I had a male mind. I just had to pretend it was female."

Julia and Betty both processed this.

A knock at the door made all the women jump.

"Julia?" It was Jack Merrick's voice. "Are you there? Is Mr. Hunter with you?"

Julia stood up. "Quickly, Evelyn. Go to my bedroom."

Evelyn did as she was bid. Julia waited until she was out of sight and then opened the front door.

Merrick stood there, slightly out of breath, his face liberally covered in soot. He was wearing an undershirt that was also filthy, and work pants, but no shirt or jacket.

"Shhh," Julia said to him, "Mr. Hunter is trying to rest."

Merrick paused for a beat. "In your bedroom?" he finally said.

"Yes," Julia stood up a little straighter and opened the door wider giving Merrick a full view of the living room, "Betty Mitchell is here chaperoning if you're worried."

"I wasn't... I, um..." He was flustered. And bothered. But he righted himself quickly. "The house is gone."

"Oh no."

"Yes. But we kept the fire off the Carson's house and it's almost out. Walt and the others are staying there, keeping an eye on it, making sure it doesn't flare up again."

"Good." Julia nodded. She felt awkward. She hadn't spoken to Merrick since their argument at the livery.

Merrick looked to Betty and then back to Julia. "Will Hunter be staying with you until he finds new housing?"

Julia thought that if he wanted the question to sound innocuous he failed. She heard Betty's voice from behind her.

"He'll be staying with Christopher and me, Constable. I'll be taking him home to feed him as soon as he wakes."

"Right." Merrick took a step back from the door. "I'll go back and see how the men are doing."

He turned and strode down the front walk. Julia secretly appreciated the view of his back clad in just his damp undershirt. She closed the door and turned, finding Evelyn Hunter in the doorway to her bedroom.

"Well, the cat's out of the bag now," her guest said, "I might as well slink out of town on the first stagecoach."

"Nonsense," Betty stood up and put her hands on her hips. "What we do next is find you one of Christopher's suits to wear."

CHAPTER TWENTY-EIGHT

Merrick found Walt with Dr. Parker out in front of the livery. The doctor was sitting on one of the old wooden chairs. He had one of the livery dogs clamped between his knees. The dog was facing in, toward the doctor. Walt was standing beside the chair and had the animal's head gently but firmly clasped between his large hands. Dr. Parker had his face bent close to the dog, examining one of its eyes.

Walt turned his head as Merrick walked toward them and nodded at his friend.

"I didn't know you saw patients with four legs as well, Doctor."

Parker grunted, focused on his task.

Walt replied for him. "I asked him to look at this fellow. He's had something wrong with one of his eyes for a few days and it's getting worse."

Merrick glanced around at the other two dogs who were lying in the yard, unaffected by the goings-on of the medical procedure. "Who do these mongrels belong to, anyway?"

"No idea," Walt said. "They just show up each morning and disappear every day at dusk."

With Walt slightly distracted, the dog tried to pull its head out of his hands. Walt turned back to the patient and spoke some Gaelic words to it in a deep calm voice. The dog stopped fidgeting.

Parker finally spoke. "Constable, hand me the small tweezers from my medical bag, will you?"

Merrick found the bag behind Parker's chair and dug around in it, coming up with a long, curved instrument with pincer ends and round handles for wielding it. "This?" he said, holding it up.

"No. There should be some brass tweezers in there. Smaller than that."

Merrick searched again, digging past a stethoscope, a thermometer, several sizes of scissors and something that looked like a spoon with a square head until he found what he thought Parker wanted. When he pulled them out of the bag and held them up Parker nodded.

"Is there a magnifying glass in there too?"

Merrick reached into the bag once more and then handed the doctor the glass.

For a few more moments the operation was quiet. Walt continued to talk to the dog under his breath. Merrick couldn't understand the words, and he supposed the dog couldn't either. But whatever Walt was saying was calming the animal.

The dog made a small whining noise and then Parker sat back in his chair, the tweezers held aloft in front of him. "Voilà," he said.

Walt released the dog's head, and the doctor unclamped his knees. The animal backed away and shook himself all over. He rubbed his face a few times with his paw and then trotted away and began pushing his head into one of his compatriot's shoulders.

"What was it?" Walt asked.

Parker turned the tweezers in his hand, examining the

offending object closely. "Part of a pine needle, I think. It was stuck in his eyelid." He flicked the needle away and stood up.

Walt shook his hand. "Thank you," he said.

"No problem, Sheehan. My pleasure."

When the doctor left, Merrick and Walt went inside and began the daily chore of mucking out the stalls. Walt placed the wheelbarrow in the center aisle of the livery and both men grabbed a pitchfork from the tack room. Merrick started with Earl's stall and Walt let himself into the stall where his horse, Nelson, normally stood. Both animals were outside, which made the job much easier.

They worked silently for several minutes. Both men were weary from being up most of the night at the fire. The smell of soot lingered in their nostrils. Eventually Walt said, "You seemed a bit short with Julia the other day."

Merrick grunted in reply and kept sifting through the straw for lumps of manure.

Walt tried again. "How is it that one woman can cause you so much aggravation? She must be magic or something."

The silence from Earl's stall stretched out.

"Maybe," Walt continued, trying to get a reaction, "you could hire her as your assistant. She could solve the crimes and you could do the paperwork."

"Why are you so chatty all of a sudden?" Merrick's tone was grave.

"Just wonderin'. She's like a fly at a picnic, that one. She won't go away no matter how much you swat at her."

Merrick looked up through the bars that divided the top half of the stalls. "Exactly! I keep telling her it is not her place to be running around town, solving crimes. She's going to get herself hurt. Or worse. I was angry because she went to the O'Brien ranch the other day. By herself, no less." Merrick bent to his task again, his face furrowed with concern and anger.

"Did she come back in one piece?"

"What?" Merrick hadn't heard Walt over the grumbling in his own head.

"I say, did she come back in one piece? Was she safe? Did she get hurt while she was out there?"

Merrick lifted a pile of poop onto his pitchfork and walked it out of the stall to the wheelbarrow. "No. She didn't get hurt. But that's not the point. She could have. The men at that ranch are dangerous. I wouldn't let any woman go out there alone."

"I suppose she didn't need your permission." Merrick grunted again at this but Walt continued. "You know, she reminds me of someone."

"Really? Who?"

"There's a man in town who's fiercely independent. Won't let his friends help him even when he's grieving and lost for what to do next. He's proud and stubborn as hell. Smart about his job but not too bright when it comes to dealing with people sometimes." Walt finished in Nelson's stall and moved across the aisle to a box reserved for guest horses.

"Very funny," Merrick said.

"I'm not being funny," Walt said. "I'm serious. You two are like peas in a pod. I think that's why she drives you mad. You see yourself in her. She's lost, like you were after Charlotte died, and she's grabbing onto a task that gives her a sense of purpose and probably distracts her from whatever's bothering her."

Merrick stood up straight and leaned on his pitchfork. "Since when did you become Aristotle?"

"Since never. I'd have to be blind not to see how irritating you find Julia. And I just got to wonderin' why."

For the third time, Merrick grunted. He continued leaning on his pitchfork, his eyes focused on nothing, deep in thought. "What am I going to do?" he finally asked. "She won't listen to reason. She won't stop interfering. I can't arrest her just for being a giant pain in my ass."

Walt stood up as well now, and looked across the aisle at his friend. "Have you tried talking to her?"

"Of course I've talked to her. I feel like I do nothing else but talk to that damned woman these days."

And then Walt said the wisest thing he'd perhaps ever said, "Aye, but have you listened?"

CHAPTER TWENTY-NINE

Julia and Betty kept their ears and eyes open for days after the fire, looking for signs that others in town had noticed James' female silhouette when he was outside his home in his nightshirt. James, who they continued to refer to in the male form, as that was his preference, was feeling the loss of his home keenly. But more than that, Julia could see he was convinced he would have to move away.

Betty had found him an old suit of Christopher's, as she'd promised, and in the early light of Friday morning, she altered it so that he could wear it that day. He was also offered the spare room in the Mitchell's living quarters, though he declined.

"I think that would be a bit awkward, Betty," James said, while standing on an ottoman so she could pin the hem of his trousers. "Christopher is a perceptive man. He'd figure out that something was going on. This is why I tend to stay out of relationships. I'll ask Walt if there are any rooms at the livery. I can't afford to stay at the Finnegan's hotel."

The watchmaker buried himself in work; he was at the store every time Julia went to check on him. He had always been a bit closed off with her, but now was even more so. He could hardly look at Julia, and soon she began to feel her presence was more of a burden than anything else.

When he wasn't working, Hunter hovered over the site where his little home had been. He had picked through the ashes and found some pieces from the clocks that were in his home; two pendulums, some gears, a clock face, twisted and melted.

On a Saturday evening in late October, Julia found Merrick and Walt in Finnegan's restaurant. Walt pulled a chair out for her as she approached.

The men were eating their evening meal in the restaurant, as they so often did. Without wives to cook for them at home, and left to their own devices, both men preferred to pay for their main meal of the day. Merrick was a dab hand at baking bread, but that was where his culinary skills stopped. Walt never seemed to care about food one way or the other. He ate what was put in front of him, and did so indiscriminately. Julia wondered how he'd grown so big without any interest in fuel.

Julia splurged and ordered the special from Caroline; leg of lamb with boiled potatoes. The men were finishing their meals. Merrick chewed a piece of ham and watched Julia remove her gloves. She looked up at him. This was the first time they'd spoken since their argument at the livery, barring the few moments at her front door the night of the fire. Julia noticed a little anxious fluttering in the pit of her stomach.

"Any idea how the fire started?" she asked, mostly because she wanted to know, but also partly because she wanted to see Merrick's reaction.

Merrick gave her a cool glance and then looked at Walt. Julia followed his gaze and saw the blacksmith arching one eyebrow at his friend. Julia wasn't sure what that was about but when Merrick spoke he seemed to be making an effort to sound calm. "Nope. But my guess is it didn't start in Hunter's wood stove."

"Why do you say that?"

"Hunter said he saw the flames out the bedroom window first. It was the crackling that woke him up. Another minute or two and he'd have been singed down to his bone marrow."

Julia shuddered at the imagery.

Merrick continued, "And the stove was one of the only things left, of course. The ashes in it were minimal. Hunter obviously kept it clean and tidy. And I've no reason not to believe him about when he saw the flames. Although we," he nodded his head toward Walt, "had a look at what was the back of the house, and couldn't see anything that indicated foul play."

Julia opened her mouth to speak, but Merrick continued.

"But, given what Hunter has been through recently, I wouldn't be at all surprised if someone started the fire. He seems to have made an enemy here in Horse." Merrick put his fork and knife down on his plate, wiped his mouth with his napkin, and leaned back in his chair. He looked steadily at Julia. "You wouldn't know anything about that, would you?"

"No, sir." She smiled, happy not to be forced to lie. She knew other things she wasn't telling Merrick, like the specifics about Hunter's gender, for example, but she was still at a loss about who meant him harm.

Merrick cast a weary glance at her. "Why do I so often get the feeling there's something you're not telling me?" He seemed less frustrated tonight and more resigned.

Julia looked over at Walt. He winked at her.

Caroline set Julia's supper down in front of her. Along with a glass of amber liquid she hadn't ordered. And a glass each in front of Merrick and Walt.

"What's this?" Julia asked.

"Compliments of Mr. Anker." Caroline stepped aside and

revealed the rancher sitting with his wife at a table tucked into a corner of the room.

The three recipients of Anker's generosity raised their glasses to him. He nodded and raised his back.

When they'd each taken a sip, Walt set his glass down and asked Merrick, "Any progress on finding Julia's attackers?"

The constable nodded slightly. "I suspect they were drifters, unfortunately. I had a telegraph message this morning about a similar happening in Lumby last night. A woman taking a walk after supper was grabbed by a fellow."

The hairs stood up on Julia's arms. "What happened?"

"Nothing, luckily."

Julia let out a breath she hadn't realized she was holding.

Merrick continued. "It just happened that this woman had her dog with her. A great big wolf-like thing, apparently. I guess the man who tried to attack her hadn't noticed the dog, but when the dog saw him touch his mistress, he launched himself at the guy and nearly tore him apart."

"Good for that dog," Walt said.

"Exactly. The dog got his message across; when Lumby's constable went to look at the location of the fracas this morning, there was blood on the ground. The woman screamed at some point and the dog let go. But whoever this guy was, he's got some wounds he'll need looked at. I've alerted the doctors in the area and south to Penticton, so maybe he'll be dumb enough to visit one of them and we can nab him."

"Just one guy this time?" Walt asked.

"They think so. Either that or number two hadn't moved out of the shadows yet, and when the dog attacked he wisely took off. Anyway," he turned to Julia who was taking a sip of her whisky, "whoever they were, I don't think they were local. I know that doesn't make it much better, but I think the chances of another attack are slim to none."

"That is some comfort," Julia said, reluctantly remembering her encounter. A thought occurred to her. "On the night of the dance, one of the men used my name. If they were drifters, how do you think they knew?"

"That's been bothering me as well. It's why I wanted to question the men at the surrounding ranches. But," he chewed the inside of his cheek for a moment, "I don't have an explanation. It was dark and you were alone, so no one else used your name while you were outside, correct?"

Julia nodded.

"My guess is that they'd seen you in town earlier in the day or on another day, and found out who you were then. I expect they were lying in wait for a woman to go alone to the outhouse. And when you appeared they were able to use your name to intimidate you. It must have been unsettling to hear it."

This wasn't a question, but Julia nodded.

"I'm sorry it happened, but as I said, I think it was an isolated event. Keep your eyes open over the next little while, though, and let me know if you see anyone resembling those men."

Julia pushed her plate away. Even though she had only eaten half her meal, her appetite was gone. She was reminded that for the past few days she had been trying to distract herself from her fears about what had happened the night of the dance by focusing on James Hunter's problems. Merrick's update brought home to her again the fear she was trying to avoid, and though it was good news that the men were probably not local, she found herself feeling unsettled.

Thankfully, a distraction arrived in the form of Gerard Anker and his wife. "Hard at work, I see, Constable." The rancher clapped Merrick on the shoulder, and smiled, teasing.

Anker wanted to know about the fire. He hadn't been there for the event and he and Mrs. Anker had just seen the blackened remains of the house as they'd driven into town that afternoon.

"Isn't it terrible?" Mrs. Anker said to Julia in her strongly-accented English. "That poor man lost everything."

She seemed to want to continue to collect any details from Julia, but her husband took her arm. "Come now, dear, we must be going." Gerard Anker pulled on his hat and a pair of deer-skin gloves, preparing for the wagon ride back to the ranch. "We need to get back before dark. I forgot to bring a lantern."

Anker shook Merrick and Walt's hands and, as he had done at the ranch, lifted Julia's hand to his and kissed her fingers.

Sabine swatted his arm playfully. "Stop flirting, Bärchen. We must be going."

The couple left, and Julia took another sip of her whisky. She curled her nose with distaste when she put the glass up to her face.

"Are you going to just grimace at that or can I have it?" Walt asked.

Gratefully, Julia pushed the glass over to him. She turned to Merrick, "What do you know of Walter Meddy?"

"The baker? When I don't have time to make my own, I like his bread. Why?"

"At the game the other night," Julia noticed herself shying away from using the word 'poker', "it was you guys who mentioned that Meddy kept losing to Hunter. I talked to him the other day..."

At this Merrick groaned. He rolled his head back and took a deep breath, and then leaned forward again.

Julia continued, undeterred by his irritation, "...and he was rude to us - Betty was with me - and he seems like a grumpy, unhappy person. But physically violent? Somehow I don't think so. He's as soft as the dough he works with. But he said the strangest thing the other night at a dinner party the Joneses had. He said that when I found out who Hunter really was, that I'd know who beat him. Does that make any sense to you?"

Merrick was still leaning forward, watching Julia with an expression of dismay on his face. When she stopped talking and looked at him, he couldn't seem to find the words to speak. They stared at one another for a moment and then Merrick said, "Do you not have a classroom to teach?"

Julia looked puzzled. "Right now? No. Of course not. It's…" she looked at the large grandfather clock that stood in one corner of the dining room, "quarter past seven. School got out hours ago."

Merrick continued to glare at her. Julia hadn't seen him quite like this before. "I don't mean right now. I mean, shouldn't you be focused on something else other than doing my job for me? You have a job, right? The city employs you to teach the children. Have I got that right?" His tone was dripping with sarcasm.

Julia fidgeted in her seat, and her color began to rise. She'd angered him again after a brief respite.

"I just think," Merrick said, "that if you're being paid to do one job, you shouldn't be gallivanting off and doing another."

"Well, I..." Julia began.

Merrick held up his right hand, stopping her. "Tell me this: Did Mayor Billy and the other town council members hire you to be my assistant but forget to tell me?" He didn't wait for an answer, barreling on, his voice getting deeper and more growly with every sentence. "Because if they did, I have a hell of a lot of paperwork on my desk that I'd like help with. Do you know how to work a telegraph machine? Because I could use some assistance on that front as well. What about brands? Do you know how to register cattle brands? I'll bet you do because you seem to know everything else about my job. How about this," he pulled his napkin off his lap and threw it on the table, "I'll take a well-deserved day off tomorrow and go hunting. You can manage the office and deal with whatever problems arise during the day. How about that? The door will be unlocked in the morning and you can just let yourself in and have a grand old time. Right? Good."

Merrick pushed his chair back and stood up. Without looking at Walt or Julia he left the table. He grabbed his hat from off the hat tree near the front door and left the restaurant, closing the door more firmly than necessary behind him.

"Oh my," Julia said, not sure whether to be embarrassed or amused. "I seem to have ruffled some feathers." She looked at Walt. "Again."

CHAPTER THIRTY

Something had been gnawing at Julia's mind all morning. She woke early, a good hour before she needed to get up. Unable to get back to sleep she went to the school early to work on lesson plans. Whatever it was that was bothering her subconscious would not come to light. She focused her attention as much as she could on the lessons, hoping that, as with an animal of prey, if she was still and quiet enough it would come out into the light. So far she'd had no luck.

Just before nine o'clock, the children began arriving. She got them settled and tried focusing on working with each of them. Elise Campbell, a normally bubbly and vivacious seven year old was fighting a cold, and had an upset stomach. After jollying the child along for a while, Julia finally gave up and let her lie down on the mat with a blanket and feather pillow she kept in the classroom for just such emergencies. The girl fell asleep almost instantly.

The rest of the morning passed as most schooldays did; she helped with problems when students encountered them, encouraged those who were not swift learners, challenged those who had the ability to stretch, and wiped a few noses. Elise's cold seemed to be threatening to sweep through the room and Julia had no doubt that in a day or two she'd be down to just one or two students, the rest laid up at home. When one person in their company got sick, the others almost always did as well.

At noon, Julia released the fidgety inmates, requesting that they spend at least twenty minutes outside. She hoped the fresh air and movement might cleanse the cold bug from some of them. When she checked on Elise, the girl was flushed, but sleeping peacefully, so she left her.

Julia sat at her desk, staring out one window, willing the tickle in the back of her mind to come forward.

"Miss?" It was John Purvis, an eleven year old with a surprising passion for math.

Julia looked up, "Yes, dear?"

John pulled his cap off as he entered the classroom, but he was still wearing his outdoor coat and gloves. "May we take the croquet set out of the shed?"

"Certainly, John. Just be sure to put everything back when I call you in."

He disappeared before she finished her sentence.

The tickle in her subconscious had gotten stronger while the boy was standing there. She felt it the way you feel a word on the tip of your tongue that you can't quite reach. She became very still, even widening her vision, looking at the wall but seeing nothing. She pictured John again; his cap folded in his gloved hands, his short leather boots, his little buttoned overcoat that was too big, a hand-me-down from his older brother, Steven.

It came.

Julia leaped out of her chair and trotted to the alcove between the classroom and the front door, where the hooks for coats and hats lined the walls on both sides. She grabbed her long wool coat and stuffed her arms into it as she ran down the schoolhouse steps.

"Katherine," she called.

"Yes, Miss?"

"Keep an eye on things for five minutes. I'll be right back."

"Yes, Miss."

RUNNING in a corset is no easy task. Julia had to slow to a walk several times on her journey, which infuriated her. But her lungs had very little room to expand under the stiff boning, and she certainly didn't want to pass out.

She finally reached the watchmaker's shop and pushed her way through the front door. She didn't notice the bell tinkling to announce her arrival.

"Mr. Hunter?" she called out.

The shop was silent. She called out again and stood still, listening. Her breath was coming hard and it was difficult to hear over it.

She slipped around the counter to the spot where she had found Hunter last time, grateful he was not there again. Immediately upon going through the door to the back of the shop, she knew she was probably too late.

Once again the workroom was in disarray. Clock gears and tools were scattered on the floor. Hunter's work stool was toppled over, lying on its side. She picked the stool up, unconsciously returning things to order.

Hunter would not voluntarily leave things in this state. She knew that.

The back door was closed, but on second glance Julia saw that it was standing just outside the frame. It was not latched.

She took three long strides and pulled the door open, stepping out into the yard. Silence. No movement.

Julia trotted all the way to the back of the yard, and glanced right down the narrow dirt track that ran behind the buildings on this stretch of Main Street. Nothing.

She glanced left.

Just turning the corner was a small wagon. She saw the

back of Hunter's head in the passenger seat, his posture stiff with fear. Beside him, Gerard Anker held the reins and drove the horse on.

"WALT!?" Julia's breath was coming in ragged gasps now, her rib cage aching to be allowed some room. She had run from the watchmaker's shop down the dirt track to the back of the livery.

Walt had left the week's Horse Gazette on the workbench in the tack room. She tore a page off the paper and grabbed a pair of scissors lying on the bench. There was a stubby carpenter's pencil there too. She grabbed that and wrote 'Gerard Anker' on the paper, running over the lines multiple times to make her words visible over the newsprint.

She had no time to saddle Stanley. The horse, as intuitive as any of his brethren, picked up on her energy and tossed his head as she fitted his bridle over his ears.

She knew Walt wasn't in the forge because there was no noise coming from that workshop. And Merrick wasn't around. She had noticed his office door was closed when she'd run down Main Street minutes earlier.

Taking Stanley's reins in hand, she walked him down the center aisle of the livery. Using the scissors, she stabbed the paper and affixed it to the livery door, much as the rabbit had been attached to her front door. Julia didn't have the advantage of a stirrup so she pulled Stanley over close to the fence that bordered the livery yard and awkwardly climbed up on the bottom rail. She threw Stanley's reins over his head and gathered them at his withers. The animal stood still, suppressing his excitement. She hoisted herself up onto his back. It wasn't pretty, but she got it done. She spent a few precious seconds adjusting her skirt; she wasn't wearing her jodhpurs. Just a pair of wool tights under her skirt. Her inner thighs would pay for that in the morning, she knew, but she had no choice. She squeezed Stanley's sides. He didn't need the encouragement. The horse leapt forward, nearly toppling Julia, but she held on, grabbing a fistful of his mane. A light touch on his right reign sent him in the right direction. They galloped down Main Street, heading out of town.

I'm definitely going to be away from the classroom for longer than five minutes, she thought. *Hopefully Katherine has everything in hand and remembers to check in on Elise.*

ANKER WAS MOST likely heading toward his ranch. Julia took the road out of town that he'd use. After ten minutes of nearly flat out running, though, she couldn't see Anker's wagon up ahead. She slowed Stanley to a trot, thinking.

In her mind, Julia pictured the Double A ranch. Where would Anker be headed if not to his home? What else would he be doing?

Spurring Stanley into a canter, she aimed him for the top of a shallow hill that was up ahead. When they reached the crest, she slowed Stanley to a walk, and then halted him, scanning the horizon in every direction. She saw several head of cattle in a field half a mile away and possibly a white-tailed deer grazing near a small stand of trees. When she turned all the way around, placing her right hand on Stanley's rump, she could see Horse laid out below her, like a drawing on a map. If she had been higher up and perhaps fifty yards to the west, she might have been able to see the Double A itself. Julia turned back and faced Stanley's ears. She had no choice but to carry on to the ranch and see if Anker was there. As she clucked Stanley into motion again, movement out of the corner of her eye caught her attention. She turned the horse so that he was facing the town and leaned forward, squinting. It looked like Anker's wagon - at least, it was a small wagon with two figures in it. It was on the opposite side of town from where Julia was, heading toward the lake.

Julia was unsure. It could be Anker and Hunter, but from this distance there was no real way to tell. She groaned aloud. Stanley flicked his ears at the sound but stayed still. The wagon kept moving, driving past the few buildings near the shoreline, until it disappeared behind the lumber yard building.

Julia waited, willing the wagon to reappear, but after what seemed like months, it did not. She groaned again, louder this time, and swore under her breath.

"Well, Stanley," she finally said, "bloody hell. I'm going to take a guess that that's Anker. Let's hope I'm right."

She tapped Stanley's sides.

CHAPTER THIRTY-ONE

By the time Julia reached the back of the waterfront building, her rear end was aching from the strain of riding without a saddle. She slowed Stanley to a walk and cautiously approached the corner of the building. Taking a chance, she slid off the horse and, walking to the edge of the building, she peered around the corner. She almost yelped when she saw Anker's wagon parked not six feet away. Backing up, she led Stanley to the front of the building and tied his reins loosely to a hitching rail there.

Anker was wheezing with the rattling breath of an asthmatic. His face was red with exertion and damp with sweat. He looked as though he could have a heart attack at any moment. He was busy pushing the row boat down the beach and didn't seem to have heard Julia approach.

Julia snuck up to the wagon where Hunter sat on the driver's bench. His complexion was blanched. He looked at Julia with eyes that were sunken into his face, his skin the pale green-yellow of someone with the flu.

Julia briefly wondered why Hunter hadn't just run while his captor was distracted, but as she approached the wagon she saw that his hands and feet were tied in front of him with thick rope. Glancing to where Anker still worked to get the rowboat down to the water, she stayed low on the far side of the wagon. Hunter's eyes grew wide when he saw her, but he kept quiet and held his hands out without prompting. Julia began to try to untie the knots. They were stuck fast and Julia could see Hunter's small wrists were being squeezed. Anker continued to grunt and strain with the small boat. Julia could hear the scrape of the bow on the sand and small pebbles of the beach. She gave a silent prayer, asking that Anker continue to be preoccupied.

The knots in the rope wouldn't budge. Julia tried putting her fingertips in the creases where the rope overlapped itself, to pry the knots apart, but made no progress. She reached down and tried working on the knots around Hunter's ankles. These were tied with less force and began to slip away. Julia pulled frantically at the rope, untangling it. Hunter squiggled his feet a bit as well, kicking them loose. The rope fell onto the beach and Julia decided that the best plan for them was just to run. Hunter would have to do this while his hands were still tied. She grabbed his elbow and made a motion with her eyes and head, letting him know they were going to make a break for it.

"Hey!" Anker's voice rang out, startling Julia, causing her to jump. "Get away from him."

Julia turned, straightening her spine, and faced Gerard Anker. She tried to steady herself. "Mr. Anker. This is ridiculous. Let Mr. Hunter go."

"Step away, Miss Thom. This is none of your business."

"It certainly is my business. I don't know what you have planned, but you need to let Mr. Hunter go right now."

Anker took a deep breath and wiped his face on his coat sleeve. The breeze off the water was cool, and Julia felt herself shiver, though she wasn't sure it was from the cold.

Very casually, as though he was reaching for a handkerchief, Anker reached into his coat pocket and pulled out a small revolver.

"Step back, Miss Thom, or I will shoot you. I promise."

Though he was sweating and red-faced from exertion, Anker did look absolutely serious. His face was filled with a fury Julia had not seen before. Still, she tried to talk him out of whatever he had planned.

"Mr. Anker, be reasonable. What on earth has Mr. Hunter done to you to make you so angry?"

"He knows what he's done." Anker stepped forward and pushed Julia aside, roughly. He grabbed Hunter's right arm and pulled him to the edge of the wagon's seat. Julia recovered her balance and stepped back toward Anker, reaching out for his left arm.

Anker whirled around and jabbed the revolver into Julia's stomach.

"I said stay back."

Julia's corset protected her from the full force of the jab, but it still hurt. She took a step back, holding her stomach and meeting Hunter's eyes.

Anker pulled Hunter out of the wagon roughly and jerked him forward. Hunter fell to his knees, and Anker yanked him up again.

Anker turned once more to Julia. "If you take one step, I will shoot you."

She believed him.

Anker led Hunter down to the shore where the rowboat sat, half-in and half-out of the water, its pointed bow rocking slightly with the motion of the lake. The two men reached the boat, and Anker roughly pushed Hunter into the vessel.

"Go to the back," he said.

Hunter climbed over one bench seat and turned around, sitting down facing the bow, and the shore. Anker glanced at

Julia and pointed his gun at her. "Remember, I've still got this," he said.

He put the revolver back in his pocket and then bent over to push the bow out into the water. The boat, heavier now with Hunter in it, resisted Anker's effort. But after two or three heaves, Anker was able to get some momentum going. Once in motion, the boat slid into the water.

Anker hopped in as the boat began to slide. He positioned himself on the bench seat opposite Hunter, his back to the bow of the boat, and reached for the oars. The little boat was bobbing in the shallow water. Julia saw that Anker would need to swing it around so that he could row away. Moving as little as possible, she unbuttoned her coat and waited until Anker's attention seemed to be mostly focused on the task of lifting the oars out of the boat and into the water. He looked awkward and uncertain in his movements. He was a rancher, not a sailor. She shrugged her coat off her shoulders and waited.

One oar clicked into its lock, and then the other. Anker pulled mightily with his right arm, on the port side, and the bow of the boat began to swing to Julia's left. She seized the moment and ran, arching wide to her left, trying to stay out of Anker's sight while the boat spun. In five running strides, inefficient because of the sand, Julia hit the water, diving to the starboard side of the small rowboat. Her dive was basically a belly flop because the water was so shallow near the store, her intention being to stay so close to the boat that Anker couldn't shoot her.

The cold of the water sucked the breath out of her lungs. She had misjudged how fast the boat was swinging around, and it hit her as she lifted her head out of the water. She struggled to swim in the path of the bow of the boat as it swung around. She could see very little of what was happening above her and her ears were full of the sound of water. The boat knocked her sideways, pushing her into the lake bottom and rolling her over slightly. Her dress tangled around her legs, the heavy cotton fabric instantly waterlogged. A wave caught Julia in the face, and she swallowed a good measure of lake water. She sputtered and coughed, trying to roll back over onto her stomach. Her right hand struck wood and she grabbed hold of the gunwale. The water was deeper now, the bottom of the lake dropping away quickly.

From above her there was shouting, and she tried to make herself as small a target as possible. The boat drifted farther out into the lake, so when Julia tried to touch down she could just barely feel the lake bottom. She grabbed the gunwale with her other hand and risked pulling herself up above its rim. Anker and Hunter, she realized, were both standing up in the boat. Hunter's hands were still tied, and he was struggling to keep hold of Anker's arms. Julia saw the metallic flash of the revolver in Anker's hand. Hunter was trying to prevent Anker from shooting one or both of them.

Julia took a deep breath and called out to Hunter as loudly as she could, "Can you swim?"

Hunter and Anker continued to wrestle, and it looked like Anker was gaining the upper hand. He was able to pull one hand free and began striking Hunter on the face with it. Because Hunter's hands were tied, he had to use them both for the task of warding off Anker's blows.

"Can you swim?" Julia called again.

But Hunter was too busy wrestling with Anker to either hear or answer.

Julia had no choice. She dropped down from above the gunwale and, positioning both hands low on the boat's side, she pushed.

The boat rocked slightly but remained upright. The men inside, however, were jostling it and rolling it with their physical momentum. Julia took a deep breath and waited, her hands in position. When the boat rocked away from her she pushed again, pressing her toes just barely into the lake bottom and using the boat's momentum to her advantage.

This time the rowboat tipped, the small keel nearly catching Julia on the chin.

The boat didn't flip over entirely, but the rocking was enough that Julia heard a splash on the far side as both men hit the water.

CHAPTER THIRTY-TWO

In the end it was Hunter that Julia had to save from drowning.

Julia swam around the stern of the boat and found Anker making a lot of noise and flailing his arms about, but he was moving toward shore decisively and Julia could tell he was in no danger. Hunter though, was another story. With his hands still tied, he was doing his valiant best to tread water. Despite all his effort, his face was barely peeking above the waterline. Julia, who was herself exhausted, swam to him, her waterlogged dress threatening to pull her under. Her breathing, as ever, constricted by her corset, she focused on staying calm and taking long smooth strokes. When she reached Hunter, he looked at her with fear in his eyes, though he tried to sound brave when he spoke.

"Go catch Anker. He'll get away."

"Don't be ridiculous. You're going to drown."

She swam up close to Hunter and put one arm around his chest. "Lean back," she said. "Try to relax."

Hunter was stiff with fright, and when he tried to do what Julia suggested he panicked as he felt the water rush up over his ears. He began to sink and Julia grabbed him, pulling him up by his jacket collar. Her legs were working madly, trying to keep them both afloat. Her teeth were beginning to chatter.

"James," she gasped, "you're going to have to trust me. Do you know how to float?"

Hunter spluttered and said something but Julia couldn't hear him.

She grabbed Hunter by the shoulders and turned him around, so that he was facing away from her again. Scissoring her legs back and forth, she managed to keep both their heads up above the water. Into James' ear she said, as calmly as she could, "It's okay. We're going to make it. Take a deep breath for me."

The man did and Julia tried to as well, but caught a small wave in her mouth.

Coughing, she waited a beat and then said, "Can you lean back? Can you just relax a bit and float?"

She felt Hunter hesitate and then felt him relax slightly.

"Good. Good, you're doing great. Keep doing that. See if you can lean back toward me, and let your legs rise up to the surface as well."

Hunter did so, but when he let his head fall back toward Julia the lake water again climbed up his face and over his ears. He startled and dropped his legs again and began to flail.

"No, James you were doing great," Julia continued to hold onto the man's shoulders. Her legs were beginning to fail her though, and she felt herself getting weaker. More and more small waves caught her in the face, because she wasn't as able to hold it up above the waterline. She knew she had a very limited time until both she and Hunter succumbed.

"Listen," she continued, trying to stay calm. "When you lie back, the water is going to come up on your cheeks. It's going to feel like your face is going to go under. But it won't. I promise. If you stay relaxed and just float, I'm going to tow you to shore. Okay?"

Hunter grunted, but Julia wasn't sure if the noise was

agreement or just physical effort. He did as she asked, hesitating at first. He leaned back and Julia could see his bound hands resting on his belly. This time, when the water encroached on his face, he stayed still.

"Great," Julia breathed, more to herself than Hunter. "That's good. Okay, let's go."

With one arm, she held onto a handful of Hunter's suit jacket. With the other she made long sweeping movements in the water, pulling them forward. She was fading fast now. The weight of her clothes and Hunter's clothes was pulling her down, almost as if someone was holding onto her waist and pulling. Her face was numb. She risked a glance back at Hunter and saw that his lips were blue.

Taking long strokes with one hand, and making them as smooth as possible, so as not to jostle Hunter, she slowly made her way toward the shore. The lake knocked her in the face now and then and she'd stop to cough and splutter. Every once in awhile she pushed her legs down and tried to find the bottom of the lake, but each time she was disappointed.

Her breath started to come in ragged gasps. She tried to lift her head to see the shoreline but couldn't focus and gave up. How was it possible they'd come out this far in the boat? It had felt like they'd only floated out a few feet but now it seemed like miles back to shore.

And then Julia began to doubt herself. It felt like they weren't making any progress at all. Her legs felt like jelly and each kick they gave was weaker than a brand new kitten's. Her dress felt like it weighed several hundred pounds. She couldn't go on. She dropped her head to the side, submerging one ear and half of her face, trying to breathe above the waterline.

"Miss Thom?" Hunter said in a weak voice.

"Yes?"

"You can let me go if you need to."

Water splashed over Julia's face. She closed her eyes and felt herself sinking.

Suddenly the water around her was roiling and churning. Her eyes flew open but she couldn't see because her face was slapped by a wave. Arms came toward her and grabbed her. She held onto Hunter, and lashed out at the figure with her free hand. It must be Anker trying to finish them off.

"Let him go, Miss Thom. It's okay. We've got you."

Her eyes cleared and she looked up. Theodore Cranna's pale skin and shock of red hair filled her eye line. She heard grunting beside her.

Cranna was in the water with her, pulling her up from below the surface. Beside her was a rowboat. She glanced right and could see Arthur Sullivan, the steamship captain, leaning over the side of the vessel and pulling Hunter out of the water. Cranna treaded water, holding onto Julia. When Sully had Hunter safely in the boat, he reached for Julia. There wasn't much elegance about it but with Sully pulling from above and Cranna pushing from below they got Julia into the boat as well. She fell onto the floor of the vessel coughing, her chest rattling with water.

Cranna pulled himself up into the boat, all gangly limbs and sharp elbows. When he got himself settled on his knees in the bow Sully began pulling mightily for shore.

"Well," Cranna said, looking thrilled and excited. "Now there's a story for a dinner party."

CHAPTER THIRTY-THREE

The fire in the stove was roaring, and Julia was sure that the dry inhabitants of the room must be roasting. But she and James Hunter were very grateful for the warmth. Julia was still shivering and her dress was fairly steaming.

They were in the parlor above the general store, and Betty had gone to get a dry dress from Julia's house. Julia sat on a wooden chair from the kitchen, a towel wrapped over her hair, and another over her shoulders. Her boots were off and her feet had made a wet spot on the hardwood floor.

Christopher Mitchell was digging around in his wardrobe, finding another suit for James Hunter to wear. James was standing awkwardly beside the stove, soaked as well, his hair flattened against his skull, his newly altered suit looking like a burlap sack. He cradled his injured arm in the opposite hand. It had not been helped by the rough handling by Anker and the dunk in the lake. His face was drained of color but at least his lips weren't blue any longer.

"This way, Mr. Hunter." Christopher emerged from the hallway and led Hunter back to the master bedroom to change. As he returned to Julia, they heard noises in the shop below and then footsteps coming up the stairs. Betty came onto the stairway landing, carrying a dress and an old pair of boots in her arms. Up the stairway behind her came Merrick and Walt.

"These were the only shoes I could find," Betty said, setting them down beside Julia.

"They're fine. Thank you, Betty," Julia smiled at her friend.

Hunter came into the room at that moment, dry and dressed in a suit that was at least two sizes too large for him.

"Well, now that I've got you both here," Merrick looked from Julia to Hunter, "would you mind telling me what the hell is going on?"

"Not yet," Betty admonished him. "Julia is going to get into some dry clothes first." She took Julia's arm and led her out of the room.

ANKER WAS SAFELY LOCKED up in Merrick's jail cell.

"He's soaking wet too, of course," Merrick said, "but I put the fire on. He'll dry out."

Hunter refused to sit. He paced up and down at one end of the room.

When Julia returned from getting changed into dry clothes, Merrick's eyes followed her to where she sat. When she was settled, on the love seat this time, she felt his gaze and looked up at him. His expression was hard and she sensed impatience from him. If he had been angry the night before at Finnegan's about her interfering, he must be fuming now.

He pulled his gaze away and looked at Betty. "May I talk to Miss Thom and Mr. Hunter now?"

Betty made a small movement with her head. "Please do, Jack. I'm going to get the kettle from the kitchen."

Julia and Hunter looked at one another. Julia had no idea where to begin. Neither, it seemed, did Hunter. They looked away from one another. The room was silent.

Merrick looked, once again, back and forth between the

two of them. "Well then, how about you clear something up for me, Mr. Hunter? Why don't you tell me why Gerard Anker had you in a rowboat with your hands tied?"

Hunter stopped pacing and met Merrick's eyes. Julia could see him thinking. She wondered where he would begin. He surprised her by starting at the most dangerous place. "Because I'm a woman," he said.

If Merrick, Walt and Christopher were shocked by this they hid it well. Walt, as usual, remained almost impassive. Christopher stood up out of his chair, "Let me help Betty with the tea."

Merrick took a breath and leaned back in his chair slightly. Julia could tell he was reflexively going to tilt the chair back, as he always did with the wooden chairs at his office and the livery. The front legs of the chair started to lift. Julia leaned over and tapped him on one knee. The legs dropped to the floor again. "Is that so?" he said.

HUNTER GAVE Merrick the shorter version of his explanation about growing up feeling like he was in the wrong body. Julia watched the constable's face and saw that he was working hard not to look shocked. And mostly succeeding.

When Hunter finished, Merrick sat thoughtfully for a few minutes. Finally he said, "That doesn't explain about Anker though. Why was he trying to drown you?"

Hunter, unburdened now and without anything more to defend against, sat down. He looked at Julia, almost as though he was seeking her permission. Then he turned back to Merrick. "He was attracted to me."

Merrick nodded slightly. "Go on."

"He was attracted to me and it bothered him. He couldn't understand what was going on." Hunter waggled his head a bit, searching for a way to explain. "I think that his body, or some part of him, was responding to the fact that I am in a female body. But of course, Anker didn't know that. All he saw was a man who fixed his watches and clocks, and someone to whom he was attracted."

"Did he," Merrick searched for a word, "...proposition you?"

Hunter shook his head, emphatically. "No. Nothing like that. It was just this weird, unspoken feeling between us. I'd often see him looking at me on poker nights. Watching me. And fighting with himself."

The kettle had boiled and the tea was steeped. Betty poured a cup for everyone and passed them around, creating a moment of distraction. Hunter accepted his tea cup and drank thirstily. Julia smiled, watching Merrick and Walt with their big paws wrapped around Betty's china tea cups.

Merrick hadn't stopped thinking. As soon as everyone was seated with tea and a biscuit he addressed Hunter again. "Was it Anker who beat you up in the shop?

Hunter began to shrug and Julia leapt in. "Yes."

Merrick raised his eyebrows at her. "Why do you say that?"

"The glove. I figured it out this morning. That's why I went to James' shop at noon." Suddenly, Julia's eyes grew wide and she looked around for somewhere to put her tea cup. "Oh my God!" She started to stand up out of her seat. "The school children."

"Sit down," Betty said, patting her friend's arm, "Millie Jones is over there, keeping an eye on them. And no doubt torturing...I mean, regaling them with tales of her summer in Paris."

"Thank goodness." Julia sat back down.

"You were saying?" Merrick took a sip of tea.

"Right. Yes." Julia gathered herself together. "Remember I found that glove in the shop?"

Merrick nodded.

"I finally realized it was Anker's. When we saw him and Mrs. Anker at the hotel last night, I noticed he was wearing a brand new pair of gloves. It didn't register at the time but something was bothering me last night while I slept and then again this morning at school. I finally put the pieces together when one of the students was fiddling with his gloves while talking to me."

"Anker had new gloves because he'd lost one at Hunter's shop."

Julia nodded.

"And the fire and the rabbit." It wasn't really a question. Merrick was thinking out loud, but Julia answered anyway.

"I suspect he is responsible for those, too. The fire to try to get rid of Mr. Hunter and the rabbit to get me to stop trying to find out who beat Hunter up."

Hunter nodded, adding, "He told me today when he was driving us to the lake that he set the fire. He asked me why I hadn't made plans to leave town after the fire. That was his intention. That was why he burned my house down. To get me to leave."

"Good heavens," Betty whispered, mostly to herself.

"Why did he take you out in the boat?" Merrick asked.

"He didn't say, but I suspect he was going to shoot me and push me overboard."

Julia could see Merrick thinking some more. She enjoying watching him think. He turned his head toward her, feeling her gaze. He looked a little startled when he saw that she'd been watching him, but he recovered quickly. "How long have you known about Mr. Hunter's...situation?"

Betty answered for Julia, "Since the fire."

Merrick nodded, thinking again, and then looked at Hunter. "You told them then?"

Hunter set his tea cup down and jammed his hands into his coat pockets. "I told Mrs. Mitchell. But Miss Thom already knew."

Merrick raised his eyebrows at her. "How?"

Julia waffled for a moment.

"Come on," Merrick said. "Out with it."

"I may have taken a sneak peek at Dr. Parker's patient files." Julia cringed a bit when she said this, knowing Merrick wouldn't like it.

He didn't. His expression froze and Julia felt like the whole room got quiet, holding its breath.

Walt made a small chuckling noise. "Go easy on her," he said under his breath.

Merrick took a deep breath in through his nose and held it for a few seconds. Julia wondered if he was counting to ten. He blew the breath out and leaned forward, picking up his teacup and taking a sip. With an unnatural sense of calm he said, "Please. Tell us about that."

Julia wasn't sure if she would rather Merrick had been yelling. This quiet approach was almost more unnerving. She tried to explain herself. "I happened to be in Dr. Parker's office the other day."

"Happened to be?" Merrick asked.

She continued, unabashed, "And it just so happened that his filing cabinet was in there, too."

"Where it belongs?" There was irony in Merrick's voice.

Julia ignored him. "I had been thinking about Mr. Hunter for days, of course," she looked up at the small person who looked like a child in Christopher's suit, "and was wanting to understand him better. The idea being that if I knew more about who he was, I might be able to figure out who would want to hurt him."

Hunter, who throughout the conversation in Betty and Christopher's sitting room had looked decidedly uncomfortable, now looked slightly more relaxed. He met Julia's eyes and nodded at her, encouraging her to continue.

"And I remembered that when we'd taken Mr. Hunter to see Dr. Parker after I found him in his shop, there was an exchange between doctor and patient that struck me as a bit odd." She looked over at Hunter. "When the doctor began to take your shirt and vest off so he could see your wounds and tend to your arm, you began to panic."

Hunter nodded, remembering.

"I had been thinking about that and it had occurred to me to wonder if you didn't want Merrick and I to see you without your shirt on." She looked back to Merrick. "So I might have taken the opportunity while I was in the office to look for Mr. Hunter's patient file." Julia stopped and waited for Merrick to explode.

The constable seemed to be absorbing this information, though his face still did not betray whatever emotions he was feeling. The room was quiet again for a few moments.

Merrick was about to speak again when Betty startled everyone by leaping into the ring. "It wasn't entirely Julia's fault. I helped her. I kept a lookout for the doctor while we were in there."

A huge grin broke out on Walt's face. "Mrs. Mitchell," he said, "we hardly knew ye."

At the same time, Julia shook her head at her friend and then turned to Merrick. "She was not there. I was on my own."

Betty objected, and Julia argued with her. Merrick's eyes bounced back and forth between the two women while they corrected one another.

"All right, all right," Merrick finally said, holding up one hand. "Let's just agree that Mrs. Mitchell may or may not have given you some aid..."

"I did too help," Betty muttered, unwilling to be left out of the adventure.

Merrick continued, "...but why don't you share what really matters. What did you find when you committed the *crime*," his eyes drilled into Julia's as he emphasized this word, "of breaking into Dr. Parker's files?"

"Nothing," Julia said.

"Nothing?"

"Correct." Julia nodded and straightened her back a bit.

Merrick waited her out.

Julia glanced over at Mr. Hunter and then continued. "What I found was that there was no file in Dr. Parker's office for James Hunter."

Merrick, who had leaned forward in his chair, leaned back again and Julia could see the wheels turning in his head. When he spoke, his voice had lost some of its ice. "And that struck you as odd."

"It did."

"Was that when you knew that Mr. Hunter was ...um, well..." The sentence dangled.

"A woman," Hunter said, smiling at Merrick, letting him off the hook.

"Er, yes. Thank you. A woman."

"No," Julia said. "I had no idea then. But it puzzled me and I did wonder why there was no file. It occurred to me that one reason Parker might hide it was that there was something in it he didn't want anyone to know."

Merrick looked at Hunter. "Dr. Parker was protecting you from thieves and busybodies, like Miss Thom, was he?"

"Well...," Hunter said, not wanting to betray his rescuer, "I did visit Dr. Parker when I first moved to town because I had, er, some female troubles. I told him of my particular...situation. And I asked him then to keep my file somewhere safe. Just in case."

Merrick raised his eyebrows at Julia and shook his head slightly with amazement and chagrin. "Just in case, indeed."

IN THE COURSE of the next hour, Merrick continued to question Julia and Hunter. He wanted to be sure he understood the sequence of events that led up to finding the two of them, plus Anker, Cranna and Sully, sitting on the beach looking drained but relieved, and all except Sully, soaking wet.

When they'd gotten to shore, Cranna had chased Anker, who was inexplicably running down the beach, away from town. He wouldn't have made it very far at all because soon the shoreline disappeared and unless he wanted to swim to freedom he would have found himself at a dead end. Cranna walked him back and the sodden group had made their way through town to Merrick's office. Betty had rushed in almost immediately, having heard what was happening, and insisted they move the meeting to her sitting room so that Julia and Hunter could get out of their sodden clothes.

Throughout the questions that followed in the Mitchell's upstairs sitting room, Merrick was both calm and professional, but he was also cool toward Julia. He only looked at her when he had to, and she keenly felt his simmering anger.

Unlike the month before when she and Merrick, with Walt's help, had worked together to understand why one of Julia's students had broken into the Mitchell's store, this time Merrick seemed unwilling to accept or understand Julia's help in finding Hunter's assailant.

The last of his questions asked, Merrick stood. He shook Christopher's hand, and then, after a slight hesitation, also Hunter's.

"I'll need you to stay in town, Mr. Hunter," Merrick said, "until Thursday when the Judge gets here. But then you're free to go."

Hunter nodded.

Merrick and Walt both nodded to Christopher and Betty. As he walked past her toward the staircase, Merrick refused to meet Julia's eyes.

CHAPTER THIRTY-FOUR

The walls were bare and the clockmaker's shop had an abandoned feeling about it. It was uncharacteristically silent, without any ticking or pendulums swinging. Julia could still smell the faint metallic scent of the clocks and their gears. She imagined that would linger for some time, or until a new shopkeeper took possession.

She found Hunter packing a crate in the rear of the shop.

"You're leaving us, Mr. Hunter?"

The clockmaker looked up from the workbench and smiled at Julia, though he looked weary.

"I think it's best, Miss Thom. I'll go somewhere where I can disappear a little more easily."

The traveling judge had come and gone. Gerard Anker was convicted of arson and grievous bodily harm and had been sent to the penitentiary in New Westminster. James Hunter was free to leave.

Julia didn't try to talk him out of this decision. Despite the acceptance Hunter had found with her and the Mitchells, and with Merrick and Walt, Julia was not naive enough to expect that everyone in Horse and the surrounding area would understand or accept who Hunter was. And, in such a small place, there was no way the secret would be kept for long.

"Where will you go?"

Hunter placed some loose gears in a small cardboard box and fitted the lid on top. "I think I'll try Kelowna. It's a growing place, and might suit me well. If that doesn't work I expect I'll go back to the coast. Or perhaps east."

Julia looked around her. The shelves in the workroom had been stripped of their clocks and watches, and looked naked in the bright light that was coming through the wide window.

"Tell me this," Hunter said, "for my own edification. Was it only Dr. Parker's file that gave me away?"

Julia thought about this for a moment. "It was a combination of things, really. Your reluctance to let anyone get close to you. Your small hands." Julia hesitated and then continued. "And I found a box of china under your bed the other day when Betty and I were tidying up your house. I didn't think much of it at the time, but later I wondered what a man was doing with such a delicate china pattern."

"You snooped," Hunter teased Julia.

"I did. I'm sorry. I shouldn't have." Julia blushed slightly, feeling embarrassed.

"My mother insisted I take that china when I left home. I told her I wouldn't use it but she wouldn't listen." He sighed and picked a few large clock pieces off the table, adding them to the crate in front of him. "I can't do anything about my hands, I suppose. You see, in the future I'd like to make sure I don't give myself away."

"You didn't give yourself away this time, James. It was bad luck that Gerard Anker had some sort of sixth sense going on. And that he felt he needed to act out about it."

"I expect there are many people in the world like Gerard Anker."

Julia nodded slightly. "Unfortunately that might be true. But all you can do is your best."

"Do you think that if you hadn't seen me panic when Dr. Parker tried to take off my shirt, and if you hadn't seen the china, you would have known?"

Though he was trying to cover it, there was desperation in Hunter's eyes. Julia's heart ached for the terrible position he was in. He had a choice to live as a woman and betray his true self. Or live as a man and risk exposure and perhaps more violence.

She considered how to answer. "The truth is, James, that we can't predict the future. Who knows what might have happened if I hadn't noticed those things? But events collided the way they did. And here we are."

Hunter gave a rueful laugh. "I won't be seeing the doctor in Kelowna, that's for sure."

Julia placed a hand on his arm. "Please take care of yourself."

JULIA LEFT Hunter in his vacant shop. He refused her help to finish the packing. As she walked away she reflected about the life we wish to live and the life we have to live. Hunter's isolation touched her deeply. She wondered what it must be like to face a future filled with uncertainty and no small measure of fear. The last few weeks had been challenging for her. Everything in her life had changed, and she started to feel like she wasn't dealing with that very well. James Hunter's situation was helping her to put things into perspective.

She walked slowly, reflecting, bundled up in her long, thick wool coat and a dark blue scarf her grandmother knitted for her years ago. The sky was such a clear blue that it almost hurt Julia's eyes. The temperature had dropped noticeably in the past few days and snow was expected soon.

Hunter was paying a high price for being himself. Julia imagined that he'd have to move regularly, and would not be able to settle in one place for any length of time. Eventually people would figure out who he was, no matter how he presented himself. For the rest of his life Hunter would be in some measure of danger. But obviously he was not willing to compromise who he felt he truly was in order to conform to some sort of societal norm. That, Julia could now see, took courage. And it made her feel a measure of kinship with him.

She thought about the price she was paying for being herself, including the dangerous situations she sometimes found herself in. She had moved to Horse in a knee-jerk reaction to her father's rejection of the idea that she could go to law school. Now that she'd been on her own for nearly two months, she could see that it was perfect and inevitable that she was here, fending for herself. There was no other way for her to live. Looking back at her years as a teenager who preferred to sit with her father in his study and discuss legal cases than drink tea and discuss baby names and wedding gowns with the other girls in the neighborhood, she could see that there was no way she could have ended up anywhere but where she was. Not the town of Horse, specifically, but some place where she was able to forge her own path without the restrictions and compromises inherent in the traditional female life her mother wanted for her.

She nodded and said good day as she passed Mrs. Campbell, but her mind was elsewhere, grasping what she was discovering to be true about herself.

And then there was the matter of her estrangement from her family. She hadn't heard from or written to her parents since she'd arrived in Horse. She wasn't ready to reach out to them yet, but she knew that day would come. Her righteous indignation could only keep her warm for so long. When she thought about it dispassionately, she knew that it wasn't her father's fault that the law schools in Ontario didn't accept women. And yet, she still couldn't help feeling hurt by his dismissal of her idea that she try to be the first. She had the mind for it, and he had the financial resources.

The biggest thing that was holding her back from reaching out to her parents was that her father had laughed at her. Julia's eyes stung at the memory. He was the person whose opinion mattered more to her than any other, and he laughed when she shared her dream with him. That had been his instinctive reaction; to think that a career in law for his daughter was a joke.

Julia sniffed and dug around in her coat pocket for her handkerchief.

Her mother might not be the most affectionate person on the planet, but Julia knew she loved her. And her father...well...he was a man of his time and one who was set in his ways. Though she wasn't ready, a still, small place inside Julia told her that she would have to make a choice between loving him for who he was or being permanently angry that he wasn't who she wanted him to be. The discovery of Hunter's true identity had also taught her this; people are who they are. We can accept them or not. But our lack of acceptance doesn't change them.

She blew her nose and wiped her eyes as she walked. Looking up, she realized she was passing Merrick's office. She knew while she had been trying to help Hunter that she'd stepped on Merrick's toes. She had been taking her confusion and frustration about her life out on him by pushing where it wasn't her place; using the mystery of Hunter's beating to distract herself from her own problems. Including the danger that she had been awakened to when the two men outside the dance had tried to attack her. Considering all she had done, Merrick had been more than gracious. She reflected that he probably should have thrown her in jail. She also knew that perhaps it was time to apologize to the man.

She crossed the street and stepped up onto the wooden sidewalk outside Merrick's office. The door didn't move when she turned the handle. Covering her eyes with her gloved hands she peered through the glass and could see the office was dark and empty.

~

CHRISTOPHER WAS ALONE when Julia entered the general store. He was behind the counter, unpacking a box of cans onto a shelf. Julia noticed he was whistling to himself and found herself cheered to hear it.

"Miss Thom!" he said, his wide smile brightening Julia's day slightly. Without being asked, he knew what she was looking for. "Betty is in the back. She'll be happy to see you."

Julia found her friend sitting at the wooden table in the storeroom, a pair of trousers in her lap and a sewing needle in her hand. Betty looked up when she heard Julia approach. She had pins pinched between her lips, which she pulled out and stuck into a small cushion on the table.

"Ahoy there," Betty said, grinning.

"Ahoy," Julia grinned back and sat down opposite Betty, enjoying the fact that they could joke about her adventure in Lake Okanagan. "You're making Christopher a suit?"

"This is for Mr. Hunter."

"Again? You'll be entirely responsible for his new wardrobe."

"I can't have him going off to Kelowna with only one suit."

"You're a good woman, Elizabeth Mitchell."

"Tell my husband, will you?"

"He seemed pretty cheerful when I came in. How are things on the financial front?"

"Actually, not too bad. I shouldn't disparage him. He's making a real effort to collect the money we're owed. He even got Horace Piling to pay off his debt entirely." Betty glanced up from her sewing and looked pleased. "Granted, it was only five dollars, but still. He was firm about it."

Julia was happy for her friend. "Were you there at the time?"

"I was here, in the back. I'm not sure if Christopher knew I was listening. I'm giving him the benefit of the doubt and assuming he didn't know and that he pressed Horace of his own accord."

"So, things are looking up? You may not have to live in a tent in my backyard."

"Not right away, anyway." Betty pulled a knot in the thread she was using and reached for the scissors to cut it off. Task completed, she poked her needle in the pin cushion and held the trousers aloft. "What do you think?"

"I think they look a hell of a lot more comfortable than the dress I'm wearing."

CHAPTER THIRTY-FIVE

"I'm not going to be able to get you to stop interfering, am I?"

Julia, startled, looked up from her desk where she was making notes for a lesson.

Jack Merrick was standing in the doorway to the classroom. She hadn't heard him come up the stairs. He pulled his hat off and stepped into the room. It was the first time she'd seen him since Gerard Anker's trial, a week ago.

After not finding him at his office the other day, Julia went to the smithy, where she found Walt's head bent in concentration over what looked like a fireplace poker. He was forming pieces of iron at the top of the handle into what looked to Julia like a pinecone. It was beautiful and more delicate than anything she'd seen Walt work on before. She waited, not wanting to disturb him. When he dunked the handle in the bucket of water by his feet she stepped forward and he noticed her for the first time.

She pointed at the poker. "That's lovely, Walt."

The big Irishman shrugged, and Julia thought he looked embarrassed. "It's nothing. Just a little something I'm playing at."

"Well, I think it's beautiful."

Walt's green eyes softened a little bit. "How can I help, Missy?"

"I'm looking for Merrick."

"Ah," Walt nodded, and looked back down at his piece of artwork. "He's gone."

"Gone?"

"Gone hunting. He needed a few days off. The judge told him to take some time for himself. Mayor Billy's looking after the office when he's not at the bank. Hopefully we won't have a stagecoach robbery or anything like that while Merrick's on leave."

Julia stayed and chatted with Walt for a while, but her mind was elsewhere. She was hurt that Merrick had left town without telling her. Not that he had any obligation to. Despite their differences of opinion, especially lately, she considered him to be her friend. Perhaps he didn't feel the same way about her.

She left the forge and walked home. Snow had fallen the day before and the town looked like it was wrapped in cotton wool. Julia pulled her coat and scarf tighter around herself, feeling lonelier than she had since arriving in Horse.

So, when Merrick showed up in her classroom several days later, she was startled, relieved and also apprehensive.

He walked into the room, looking like a giant among the small school desks. He walked up the left side of the room and settled his bottom on the window sill closest to Julia's desk.

"How was your hunting trip?" she asked.

Merrick nodded. "Fine. Got an elk. That'll keep me for the winter."

Now it was Julia's turn to nod. She felt anxious, and the ferocity of the feeling surprised her. She began to speak, but Merrick got in ahead of her.

"Here's what I need to know. Were you always like this? Torturing the local constabulary?" Julia thought this was an attempt at a joke, though the question sounded not-quite light-hearted.

Julia felt her defenses coming up, despite the weak attempt at humor. She pushed her chair out from her desk and turned in her seat, looking at him. "Do you feel tortured?"

"Somewhat. You see, technically I'm the one who's supposed to be solving the crimes." The look on Merrick's face was one she had not seen before. He looked calm but also a bit sad.

Julia took a breath and remembered her new expectation of herself to remember that she was not the only person in the world with concerns and beliefs about the way things should work. "I apologize," she said. "I have been putting my nose in where it doesn't belong."

The constable stretched his long legs out straight in front of him and crossed them at the ankles.

Julia braced herself for a lecture, and perhaps even the threat of charging her with interfering with an investigation. Instead Merrick surprised her. "It must be frustrating to not be able to do the type of work you want to."

Julia was more stunned than she'd been in recent memory. To her mortification, her eyes began to sting. "What on earth made you say that?"

"Walt gave me a bit of a talking to the other day." Merrick smiled grimly at the memory. "He suggested perhaps I've been too hard on you."

Julia cleared her throat. "Not really. I shouldn't be interfering with your work. You were right to tell me to step back."

"I might have been right in the eyes of the law, but I wasn't being a good friend. And that matters to me as much as being a constable. I think..." Merrick paused, and took a breath. He started again, "I had lots of time to think about things while I was away. And as much as I hate to admit it, I think my ego was bruised."

Julia breathed out a little sigh.

"Hard to believe, I know," Merrick continued, "we men are fragile creatures, Julia Thom. You're a force to be reckoned with and I think you need to be a bit patient with me. I'm just going to need some time to adjust to your...habits."

Now it was Julia's turn to smile, though hers was tinged with sadness. "I promise to try to stay out of your way from now on."

"Please don't."

She looked at him with questions in her eyes. "What do you mean?"

"You mentioned the other day that you wanted to be a lawyer."

Julia nodded.

"And you obviously have a knack for untangling puzzles. I...I don't quite know how to say this. I'm not a very eloquent man. All this trouble with James Hunter made me see something I hadn't seen before. It can't be easy to live a life that's not your own. It's not Hunter's fault he was born in the wrong type of body. There's a lot about him that I don't understand, but what I do believe is that he didn't choose the circumstances he finds himself in. And, in a similar way, it's not your fault you weren't allowed to go to law school because you're a woman."

Julia nodded again. She was struck dumb by the nature and direction of this conversation. The room almost swam around her. Outside she heard a crow call in a raspy voice.

Merrick continued. "I supposed what I'm saying is, I'm going to try very hard not to object so strenuously to your assistance from now on, should it be needed. I'm buried in paperwork and administrative duties so often that another set of eyes and ears will only make my job a little easier. Does that appeal to you at all?"

The schoolteacher nodded. She didn't trust her voice enough to speak.

Merrick continued. "All I ask is that you try not to be too obvious about it when you're helping me. And that you keep me apprised of what you know and what you're doing."

Julia nodded again. She was having trouble getting enough breath into her lungs. Not since the last time she and her father had had a debate about one of his cases in his home office had she felt so validated. She looked at Merrick and smiled, wishing she could find the words to tell him how much she appreciated that he could see her.

He continued. "And I also want to say I'm sorry."

Julia swallowed, frowning at him, confused. "Why?"

"I was hard on you the other night at Finnegan's. All I could see was that you were trying to do my job. I owe you an apology."

"I'm not trying to do your..." she began.

Merrick cut her off. "I know that. You're just trying to help. I can see that now. It's who you are. You're not interfering to spite me, or to prove me wrong. You want the same results I do." He stood up off the window sill and put his hat on.

Julia could hardly fathom what had just happened. She sat with a dazed expression on her face.

The constable walked down the length of the room and stopped at the doorway. He turned back to look at her. "C'mon. Walt and I want to buy you a pint at Finnegan's. We need to celebrate a closed case."

Julia stood up. She took her coat off the rack in the back corner of the room and pulled it on. Merrick held the front door open for her and closed it behind her as they walked down the steps.

Collecting herself, Julia said, "What happened?"

"What do you mean?"

Julia reached the ground and turned to look at Merrick. "What brought on this change of heart?"

He thought for a moment, casting his glance across the schoolyard. "That big Irishman said something to me the other day that kept ringing in my ears while I was out hunting. I couldn't get his stupid voice out of my head."

"What was that?"

"Don't tell him I gave him credit for this." Merrick now glanced at Julia.

"I promise," she said.

Merrick took a deep breath, "He said that you and I are more alike than we are different." There was a slight pause and then he concluded, "And I think he's right."

Julia's heart sang a little, and she felt a weight that she hadn't known was there lift off her chest. They walked on, boots crunching pleasantly on the skiff of snow that glazed the road.

She glanced sideways at Merrick and grinned at him, the tension of the past few days and weeks breaking. "So Walt thinks you'd look good in a dress?"

Merrick guffawed. "That's exactly right. Good luck finding a corset to fit me though."

ALSO BY ALEXANDRA AMOR

Freddie Lark Mysteries

Lark Lost

Lark Underground

Historical Mysteries

Charlie Horse

Horse With No Name

The Outside of a Horse

Water Horse

The Horse You Rode In On

A One Horse Open Sleigh

Juliet Island Romantic Mystery

Love and Death at the Inn

Children's Animal Adventure Novels

Sugar & Clive and the Circus Bear

Sugar & Clive and the Bank Robbery

Sugar & Clive and the Movie Star

Larry at the Wedding (A Sugar & Clive Novella)

Memoir

Cult, A Love Story

Alexandra Amor is a lifelong explorer of what it means to be human.

For over 20 years Alexandra has been writing both fiction and non-fiction books, all with the themes of love, connection, and the search for understanding. She began her writing career with an Amazon best-selling, award-winning memoir about ten years she spent in a cult in the 1990s.

A former Vancouverite, Alexandra now lives in a magical fishing village on Vancouver Island and spends each day writing and creating. When she's not doing that you'll likely find her walking on a beach or worrying that the vacuum cleaner feels ignored. In her spare time she serves on the boards of her local hospice association and seniors' independent living facility.

Learn more at AlexandraAmor.com

ACKNOWLEDGMENTS

Copyedit by Dawn Nassise
Cover design by Streetlight Graphics
Thanks as always to Bob Sirrine for his amazing proofreading skills.